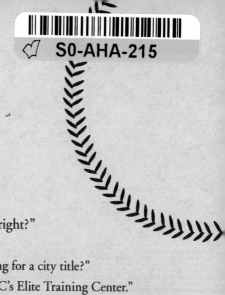

"YOU'RE A GOOD BASEBALL player, right?"

"I'm good. Yeah."

"On some big travel team? Playing for a city title?"

"With the chance to get into USC's Elite Training Center."

Trevor nodded vigorously. "All right. So, I've got something that's going to sound crazy, but I want you to think about it. I want you to think about how great it would be for you and for me."

Sam squinted at Trevor. The fancy house and pool and the maid and pool house, along with the eager look on McKenna's face, made him feel like a fly in a spider's web.

"What would?" Sam asked.

"I want us, you and me . . . to trade places."

PINCH HIT

TIM GREEN

HARPER

An Imprint of HarperCollins*Publishers*

Library of Congress Cataloging-in-Publication Data
Green, Tim, 1963–
   Pinch hit / by Tim Green. — 1st ed.
      p.   cm.
   Summary: "When movie star Trevor and regular Little League player Sam dis-
cover that they are identical twins who were separated at birth, they decide to trade
places for a while so that Sam can live the Hollywood life and Trevor can play base-
ball"— Provided by publisher.
   ISBN 978-0-06-201247-0 (pbk.)
   [1. Brothers—Fiction.   2. Twins—Fiction.   3. Identity—Fiction.   4. Base-
ball—Fiction.   5. Actors and actresses—Fiction.   6. Family life—California—Los
Angeles—Fiction.   7. Los Angeles (Calif.)—Fiction.]   I. Title.
PZ7.G826357Pin   2012   2011053346
[Fic]—dc23   CIP
                                                                                  AC

Typography by Cara Petrus
14 15 16   CG/OPM   10 9 8 7 6 5 4
❖
First paperback edition, 2013

For the Wolkoff boys,
Judah, Jacob, and
Benjamin

1

TREVOR

The warrior raised his battered and bloody sword.

Trevor was just turning thirteen, but even though his chin trembled, he looked the bearded bandit in the eye and shouted, "You can kill me, but you'll never rule this land!"

He grasped the enormous ruby from the center of the golden dragon's breast. Before the swordsman could swing, Trevor threw the jewel into the pool of orange lava below.

"CUT!"

The camera rolled back on its tracks and the boom microphones flew up and away with the wave of nearly unseen poles. The stage quickly buzzed to life with people: gaffers, artists, best boys, interns, grips, production assistants, audio technicians, and costumers. Two assistants relieved the Mongol warrior of his helmet and sword, and he clanked off in the rest of his armor toward his dressing room.

"That's a wrap for the day!" Pierce Everette, the director, shouted before he slipped up alongside Trevor. "Beautiful. You were beautiful."

Trevor didn't want to be beautiful, but he knew the director didn't mean it quite that way and he didn't stop to argue; it was his birthday, and his mother had promised him a big surprise. He thanked the director while the costume people buzzed around him, removing his armor, sword, and a small knife. Then he retreated to his own dressing room to get cleaned up and into some jeans and a T-shirt. Gabriel, Trevor's personal assistant, stood in the corner. Gabriel was tall and thin with short blond hair plastered to his head so that it looked the same no matter what the wind or weather. He wore a tailored gray suit and a face like he'd eaten a lemon. Trevor ignored him.

There was a knock, and McKenna Steele slipped inside. She had hair as black as a crow's wing. Her green eyes looked like glittering jewels in her pretty face and could only be outshone by her smile. She was tall for a girl, and thin, but she moved like a willow branch in a light breeze.

"I'm changing, McKenna, jeez," Trevor said.

"Cut it out. You wanna play Halo Reach?"

Trevor liked McKenna, maybe not in the way she liked him, but he still liked her. His mom encouraged him to spend time with her, saying there weren't a lot of kids his age who understood what it was like to be a star. McKenna certainly understood that. Although her family wasn't in the business and they weren't as rich as Trevor's, she was on the cover of the teen magazines even more often than he was, and that was saying something.

"My mom's got some surprise for me," Trevor said. "I've got to get home."

"Oh yeah, happy birthday to you."

"Don't sulk. Tomorrow."

"You always say that, but you never play Halo," McKenna teased. "I think you're afraid I'll beat you."

"Of course you'll beat me." Trevor glanced in the mirror to be sure all the makeup was gone. "I don't play it enough to beat you, but maybe tomorrow."

"Well, happy birthday for real, then." McKenna kissed his cheek, leaving.

Trevor blushed, but waited until she was gone before he brushed it off. Then he headed out himself, Gabriel following three steps behind until Trevor told him he had everything he needed and that he'd see him tomorrow.

A long limousine waited on the lot just outside the studio's airplane hangar door. The director's cousins from Cincinnati stood in a tight cluster—the ten- and thirteen-year-old girls giggling and jumping up and down, asking if they could take a picture. Trevor forced a smile and let them crowd around him. He signed a slew of eight-by-ten glossy face shots, then slipped into the long, dark car for the seven-minute ride home, happy to be alone with Dolph, the silent driver, and the dog, Wolf.

Most people freaked out when they saw Wolf, a hundred-pound German shepherd. The dog was something his mother insisted on. While Wolf could be ferocious, Trevor knew the animal was highly trained and wouldn't hurt anyone unless Dolph told him to. But just the sight of the dog kept the crazy grown-ups with cameras—the paparazzi—from swarming too close to him.

At home, Thomas, the butler, opened the front door. Behind him stood a fourteen-foot white marble statue of some Greek god. A bird flew in through the front door with Trevor. The butler gasped and followed it with his eyes as it rose up toward the domed ceiling to chirp among the painted angels and clouds, dropping a mess directly onto the head of the Greek god with a soft spatter.

"Birds!" Thomas spoke through his teeth, and Trevor stifled a laugh.

He circled the statue, then plunged through the house looking for his mother. He found her sitting in the breakfast nook that overlooked the rose garden, texting someone on her phone. Her eyes scanned the message until she saw him and focused. "How was the shoot?"

"Good. He said 'beautiful.' I don't care." Trevor spoke fast. If his mom said he'd love his birthday present, he knew he would. She wasn't given to overexaggerating. "What's my surprise?"

She fired off one more text, then cleared her throat.

2

SAM

The Ferrari fooled people.

No one would ever imagine that the people who rode in a car like that would live in an old trailer next to the dump.

The stink of the county landfill outdid any smell Sam could describe. It sat, like an unwanted guest, not in his nose, but in the back of his throat. It left a taste that stayed with Sam the entire long bus ride to school. In the summertime, though, with school out, Sam got no relief unless he went on his father's endless pitch meetings with film studios, production companies, and talent agencies. So, to escape the awful taste, Sam got up with his father, and the sun, leaving their broken trailer in a cloud of brown dust.

The fancy-looking car shone bright red and growled down the 110 Freeway as they passed Dodger Stadium. At a light on

Wilshire, the engine began to clunk. Sam looked at his dad with disapproval.

"Not again," Sam said.

"It's a delicate machine," his father replied.

"Shouldn't you sell this thing, Dad? We could move into one of those condos by the design school. They have a pool."

"A bed, a shower, a kitchen, a good pipe, and a desk," his father said with a practiced smile, "that's all you need. A Ferrari makes an impression, Son, and I'm in the business of impressions."

"You're a writer, Dad," Sam said, "and a teacher. Writer first."

His father patted the script that he'd inserted between his seat and the stick shift. Typed in big, bold letters were the words: "*Dark Cellar* by Randall Palomaki."

"Writers in the business have to look the part, and when I sell *Dark Cellar*, we'll get a house in West Hollywood where you can see forever. And a pool. Son, when your mother died, I made myself a promise. I was going to go for the gold. You understand? You don't remember Sandusky, Ohio—you were too young—but when we left, we left for good, and I will never look back."

Sam said no more, but he couldn't help sneaking a look at his father as they lurched into Paramount Studios. The guard gave them instructions where to park. Sam felt embarrassed for his father when he saw the guard smirking at the Ferrari as it sputtered away trailing a plume of blue smoke.

Sam's father parked, got out, and patted the hood of the car. "Temperamental, but a timeless symbol of success. You want to

6

be a player in this town? You gotta look like a player."

He tugged at the cuffs of his shirt, straightening the links and smoothing the sleeves of his only suit.

Sam's dad taught seventh-grade English in a poor district of LA, but looking like a middle school teacher was no way to sell a screenplay. To sell a screenplay, his dad had told him time and again, you have to *look* like you know how to play the game of life, and win. So, he had spent every cent he could possibly spare on the expensive dark suit that matched his eyes, a pair of slightly used five-hundred-dollar shoes, and a car worth twice as much as their home—a car he polished to a shine the night before even the most low-level meeting.

To Sam, pitch meetings were like pennies. If you had enough of them, they could probably add up to something, but each one held so little value that it was hard to get excited about. Still, Sam's dad plowed on, writing and rewriting script after script, determined to create the next great horror flick. Since he could remember, Sam had heard the same optimistic exclamation hundreds, if not thousands, of times: "This is it! This guy gets it. He believes in this script. We're going to get a *deal*, the green light, any day now. Any day."

So far, the deal hadn't come, but the pitch meetings continued, and his dad swore *Dark Cellar* was the ticket.

Maybe a better comparison would be a *lottery* ticket, Sam thought. Very unlikely to pay off, but if one ever did, it would be some kind of payday.

"Sam." His father stopped short and pointed at a small sign posted on a battered metal door.

"So?" Sam said. He raised a copy of *The Count of Monte Cristo* to show his dad that he had plenty to keep him busy without being a face in the crowd on some movie set. The nice thing about the studios was that they all had benches parked under shady trees spread across their lots. Sam could get a lot of reading in while his father pitched scripts.

"So, *you*," his dad said. "I'll be in town every day this summer anyway with pitch meetings for *Dark Cellar*. You could make a few extra bucks."

"I've got baseball, too, Dad."

"Not till after dinner. Sam, think of the opportunity. When I do this deal, I want you to have a role in it. If you have some experience, it'll only make it easier to convince the director."

Sam studied his father's thin face, the short, wiry orange hair and matching mustache and the freckles that went from his face all the way down his neck. Given Sam's milky white skin and long, straight, hayblond hair, no one ever confused them for father and son. "Can I use some of the money to buy that new Nike mitt? I think it'll make it easier for me to snag those line drives."

"That's the spirit!" his father said. "You go up and get the papers. When I'm done, I'll stop back by and sign whatever I have to. Sound good?"

"I'll be here," Sam said, and he swung open the door as his dad hurried off.

Beginning to climb the metal flight of stairs, Sam saw two people coming down. One had a face Sam recognized from television, and the actor's name was on the tip of his tongue, a tall cowboy with a gray beard. The second person was a woman with black plastic glasses, a sharp nose, and bright red hair. There was barely room for them to pass each other because the woman was wide and didn't try to move aside.

Sam leaned into the railing, but as they went by, he slipped and stepped on her foot. The woman tumbled down the last three steps, landed square on her big butt, and let fly a thunderclap fart. Her face went as red as her hair. The cowboy tried not to laugh, but Sam couldn't help himself.

"Why, you little brat!" The woman's voice echoed through the stairwell and Sam hurried away, pressing a fist against his mouth to muffle his laughter.

As the door swung closed behind him, Sam heard her say, "You'll get yours, you clumsy little fool."

Sam found the line of applicants. It stretched down an entire hallway. He got into it, still chuckling to himself and thinking how glad he was that he'd never see the woman again. When his turn finally came, Sam put on a serious face and stepped in front of a camera to have his picture taken. He gave his height, weight, and name before being handed an application and pointed toward a cluster of tables. Sam filled out the paperwork with the exception of his father's signature, then opened *The Count of Monte Cristo*. He figured his dad would show up soon.

He was reading when a man in a suit and tie came out from the back and shouted, "Sam Palomaki? Is Sam Palomaki here?"

Sam stood up and raised his hand while everyone stared.

"Why don't we have your application?" the man asked, obviously annoyed. "You had your picture taken."

Before Sam could answer, the man said, "Come with me."

Sam grabbed his application and held it up, hoping he could make everything okay, but the man didn't look back. Sam followed him through a doorway in the back of the room and down another hallway, feeling certain he'd spoiled any chance for becoming an extra and making the money for that mitt, and wondering if it all had anything to do with the farting woman who had been so angry.

They passed by a secretary, and the man pushed open the door to a corner office looking out over the lot. "Here. Sit down."

Sam sat down in a chair facing the polished desk, still holding the application.

The man squinted at the application, then at Sam. "Don't you know why you're here?"

3

TREVOR

"You wanted to play baseball, right?"

Trevor nodded.

"And that's what you're going to do. It's your father's and my birthday present."

"Real baseball?" For the past two years, Trevor had begged to play on a travel baseball team, or at the very least in a local league.

"As real as it gets." She smiled that famous smile he sometimes saw on billboards advertising her latest films.

Trevor's mouth dropped like a bomb. In a life of extreme privilege, it was a rare thing to be surprised or excited, and nearly impossible to be both at the same time, but this was it. He nodded his head.

"When?" Trevor spouted his words. "How?"

"It's a surprise. Now, go get that smelly glove and let's go."

Trevor's throat tightened. It didn't even bother him that before the last word left her mouth, his mom was opening another message on her phone. He hurried back into the entryway, where a worker was already up on a ladder cleaning the statue's head with a sponge. Trevor ran up the long sweeping staircase that curved around the marble entryway and then down a long hall.

His bedroom was far away, on the opposite end of the house, but he still beat his mother to the dark blue Bentley waiting for them just outside the ten-car garage. Trevor couldn't see his own personal batting cage behind the garage, but he knew it was there. He could find his way to it in the dark. He felt a pang of thankfulness for all the time he'd spent there, because today his endless hours of practice would finally pay off. The Bentley's chrome gleamed in the California sunlight, and the car sat softly rumbling, delivered to the spot by one of more than a dozen workers—mostly unseen—who cared for every detail of the massive estate.

Trevor's mother climbed in, wearing big white sunglasses and a silk scarf tied about her blond mane of hair. She took time to refresh her red lipstick in the mirror before frowning at his cleats.

"Those things in this car?" she said.

Trevor shrugged. "You need them to run the bases."

His mother shrugged back and put the big boat of a car into gear. She called into her office on the speakerphone and had her assistant begin to connect her to the calls on her phone sheet. Trevor wiggled in his seat, but then sat rigid after they passed Beverly Hills High School and every park between their

Bel Air home and the 101 Freeway. If he was going to join a league, those were the places he'd have to go. He glanced at his mom, fearing she was too engrossed in her phone conversations to remember where they were headed.

When they got on the freeway heading south, Trevor looked back over the seat at the Hollywood hills disappearing behind them, then up ahead at downtown Los Angeles.

"Where are we going?" he asked, wondering if in fact they *were* going to some special place where a travel team might be practicing.

It was almost too good to be true, but Trevor pinched his arm and knew it wasn't a dream. He was a kid people said had everything: money, fame, a loving family. But all those things had been given to him. Trevor wanted to *compete* for something, to use his own skills to try and win. And, if he didn't win, he would *lose*, and that would be okay once in a while. No more scripted lines and parts written just for him, but a real battle on a real team.

Trevor didn't spend much time with his father, and they almost never played sports. One time, though—when his father had been delayed for an afternoon trip to London because a part had to be replaced on his jet—the two of them had gone out into the yard with two gloves and a ball. Trevor had a glove signed by A-Rod, but Trevor's dad had a glove that was old and faded and well-worn. It turned out to be his father's own mitt, a mitt he had used as a player for the college team at Yale. Trevor never knew his father had been an athlete, and when Trevor threw well—earning a smile and some praise from his father—he made up his mind at that moment that baseball would be his sport, too.

Since that afternoon he'd dreamed of it, of playing, being part of a team, hitting home runs, making outs. Maybe one day he'd even play for Yale. But all his life there were reasons why he couldn't. No time. Family travels. Too much of a distraction from his work as an actor. Too difficult to deal with all the drama that came from being a kid who was not only a movie star, but the son of a movie star and a famous Hollywood producer.

Trevor's mother didn't seem to have heard his question, so he asked it again. "Where are we going?"

She clucked her tongue, muted the phone on her agent, and shook her head. "A surprise from your father and me."

"But I'm playing baseball?"

"I said you were. Relax. You only turn thirteen once. I said it's a surprise. Where we're going is part of the fun." His mother checked her lipstick again in the mirror and tucked the bra strap on her shoulder back into her shirt. She took the mute off and started talking again.

When they got off the freeway at the exit to Dodger Stadium, he knew it couldn't be a coincidence. They circled the stadium, then drove right up to the front of the team offices. His mom parked where it said "No Parking," got off her phone call, and got out while two different camera crews surrounded the car.

"What are these guys doing?" Trevor asked.

"Your father wanted to see it all," his mother replied. "Come on, pretend they're not there."

Trevor's father was on location in Australia. His studio was

14

shooting a blockbuster with Russell Crowe. Having a film crew hovering around him wasn't anything Trevor hadn't seen before, and even though it was annoying, it didn't distract him for more than a few seconds. He followed his mother through the offices, where they picked up two men and a woman, all wearing suits and fussing over his mother while saving plenty of smiles, chuckles, and nods for him. His mother didn't give them much attention in return. She began sending text messages and appeared—at the same time—to have her sights set on the field.

When they walked out onto the grass, Trevor blinked and shielded his eyes from the sun. His mind swirled with the possibilities of just what kind of travel team could possibly have the clout to practice at Dodger Stadium. And he knew it must be some kind of a travel team since they already passed by all the schools and parks near where they lived.

Out on the diamond, figures swayed in the heat. A cloud passed in front of the sun. Trevor lowered his hand and blinked.

What he saw made his stomach clench like a boxer's fist.

4

SAM

"Do you know who you look like?" the man asked. "I'm sorry, my name is Donald Fuller. I'm VP of Central Casting. Do you?"

"I know I don't look like my father," Sam said, feeling foolish.

"Your father?"

"I was waiting for him to sign that part of the application. I'm sorry. He's at a pitch meeting."

Fuller nodded. "You look like Trevor Goldman. The blue eyes. Blond hair. That long straight nose."

"Trevor Goldman? Me?"

"Do me a favor, will you? Pull your hair back off your face. Use your hands."

Sam didn't quite understand until Mr. Fuller showed him. Sam did it, pulling his hair back like he was going to put it into a ponytail. Fuller just stared.

"It's scary," Fuller said in almost a whisper. "It's unbelievable,

16

and you could wear a hairnet or a wig. You know what a stand-in is?"

"Not really." Sam wrinkled his face at the mention of a wig. "Like an extra?"

"Like an extra, but more. A lot more. You get paid ten times what an extra gets paid, and you look enough like Trevor Goldman that I want to sign you up for *Dragon's Empire*. You heard of it?"

Sam shook his head. "I've heard of Trevor Goldman, though."

"Of course you have. *Dragon's Empire* will be his next blockbuster. The stand-in we had got sick. The computer spit you right out. Same height, weight, facial features—it's all done electronically—and now that I look at you, whoa, you could be twins. Your skin is a little pale and your hair's too long, but that won't matter for a stand-in."

"What is a stand-in?"

Fuller looked to make sure Sam was serious. "You just stand in for the star while they're setting up the shot."

Sam nodded. "Like when you bat for someone, a pinch hit?"

"Kind of, but that's baseball; this is the movies. It's kind of boring, truthfully, but the money's big, big, big, especially on a blockbuster like *Dragon's Empire*. So, are you in?"

Sam started to wonder if the money was big, big, big enough to buy them that condo by the design school, but before he could ask, there was some commotion outside and a loud knock at Fuller's door. Sam's dad appeared. His red face had turned hot, and his nose shone like a stop light.

"You don't just take someone's son away and meet with him behind closed doors," Sam's father said, stepping into the room and standing rigid. "I know how things work around here. I'm at a pitch meeting with *this* studio, and I come back and someone's trying to cut a deal with my son? I'm a player in this town."

Fuller was on his feet. "Mr. Palomaki? It is Mr. Palomaki, isn't it?"

"I said I was the boy's father."

"Mr. Palomaki, I'm sorry, it's just that he looks so much like Trevor Goldman and we're shooting *Dragon's Empire* and the stand-in got sick and Sam popped up on the computer. I ran right out to get him because the studio's in a bind."

At the mention of the studio, Sam's father settled down a great deal and he put a hand over his heart. "If I can help the *studio*, I'm happy to do it. After the meeting I just had, I think I'll be working on my own project here in the very near future."

Sam secretly rolled his eyes because he'd heard his father talk big so many times before, even though nothing ever came from it.

"You got a green light?" Fuller's eyebrows shot up. "That's wonderful."

Sam's father cleared his throat. "Not quite a green light, but very close. They're talking about the terms of an option right now."

Sam looked at the floor and shook his head, but not so anyone would notice.

"Ah," Fuller said, seeming to know quite well what that meant.

"So," Sam's dad said, putting a hand on Sam's shoulder. "A stand-in? Not bad. He does look like Trevor Goldman. I should have thought of that."

Sam could almost see the wheels turning in his father's head. They could pick up some extra money *and* do the studio a favor.

"Look? I swear, without the hair, they could be twins," Fuller said.

"They say everyone has a look-alike," Sam's father said. "How long is the shoot?"

"June and July."

"Day rate?" Sam's dad licked his lips.

"Better. Background performer. Time and a half. That's two hundred a day, a thousand a week, guaranteed."

"Make it double time." Sam's dad scowled. "You said 'twins.' Think of what it'll save you on lighting and makeup."

Fuller ground his teeth and picked up his phone.

5

TREVOR

The entire LA Dodgers team stood in a group near the pitcher's mound. They broke into polite applause when they saw Trevor. One of the cameramen circled him, getting his reaction in a kind of three-sixty scene. The other took a wide shot that included his mom. Trevor's mom slipped the phone into her purse and clapped her hands like a child as she bounced up and down with excitement.

Trevor regained his wits and squeezed out the best smile he could muster.

"You want baseball?" His mom grinned so hard her sunglasses shifted on her face. "We give you baseball, angel."

"It's great, wow, meeting the Dodgers." Trevor tried hard not to sound disappointed in front of the cameras; it wouldn't be polite.

"You're not going to just meet them!" His mom's voice

continued to rise with enthusiasm and volume as she expertly turned her face toward the cameras. "You're going to *play* with them!"

"Great." Trevor kept the smile burning. "Wow. Okay. Great. Ready?"

His mom waved a finger in the air and like magic, half the Dodgers went to their places in the field while the rest of the team headed for the dugout.

"The Dodgers versus the Dodgers with Trevor Goldman!" Trevor's mom shouted, holding up a single finger.

Chad Billingsley, the Dodgers' top pitcher, called out from the mound. "You're up, Trevor. Let's see what you got."

Trevor's mom and the rest of the adults, including the camera crews, chuckled and hooted like everyone was in for some real fun. Trevor choked out a laugh and picked up the nearest bat against the fence. Don Mattingly, the Dodgers' manager, emerged from the dugout, handing Trevor a different bat.

"You're leading us off, so use this. It's from the '06 series, a little gift from me and the team. Go get 'em, kid."

The Dodgers in the dugout gave Trevor thumbs-ups from their seats. Trevor swung the bat, loosening his shoulders as he approached the plate. Rod Barajas, the catcher, smacked his glove like the real thing. "Get 'em, Trevor."

Trevor had to admit that when he stepped into the box and Billingsley went into his windup, he felt a real thrill. Even that fizzled, though, when the pitch came on a slow lob right down the middle. Trevor swung instinctively, connected, and took off like a shot. He had good speed, but even as he sprinted down the first-base line, he could see Rafael Furcal, the shortstop, snatch up the ball. After a moment he pretended to fumble with it, then drop it before scooping it back up. Trevor's foot slapped the base, and Furcal fired the ball.

"SAFE!"

Trevor was stunned to see a real umpire, decked out in his official uniform as if it were a live Major League game.

"Almost got him!" Furcal shouted.

"Kid's good," said James Loney, the first baseman.

Trevor's face felt hot with embarrassment, but he played along, running the bases until he scored and everyone cheered. Several of the Dodgers on Trevor's team met him at home plate, clapping and mussing his hair on the way back to the bench. His mom clapped wildly, walking along beside them.

The director of the camera crew approached and asked, "Can we do that again, only this time get him sliding? And maybe they could make a throw to home, and Trevor could slide just under it. I think that would be something to remember, and I know your husband would love that."

Trevor caught his mom's eye and shook his head with a pleading look. The whole thing was bad enough without having to stage him sliding into home plate.

"That's okay, Louie," his mother said, waving him off and taking the phone out of her purse so she could get back to work. "Let the boys play. Just get what you can."

Louie hung his head, but went.

After Trevor scored, the rest of his team promptly struck out.

"What position, buddy?" the manager asked.

Trevor started to say he'd go wherever they needed him, then stopped himself. They didn't *need* him anywhere. To get the whole thing over with, he said, "How about second base?"

"Trevor's got second!"

Trevor's team jogged out onto the field.

"Great."

"Let's shut them down."

"Shut them *out*."

Three times in a row, the pitcher laid in a pitch and the batters dribbled grounders right at Trevor. When he threw them out at first, everyone cheered. After the final out, everyone cheered louder and for real. Trevor's teammates slapped his back and shook his hand all the way to the dugout. Louie and his crew circled the bunch, recording it all. Trevor did an acting job for his father, grinning at the camera and pumping his fist. He knew anything less and his mother would insist that they do it again to please his father.

His mother hugged him and the entire team circled around him for a photo, then they all shook his hand again and filed into the clubhouse without a word.

"Well," his mother said, taking a deep breath and letting it out, "what did you think of that?"

"Incredible, Mom. Thank you. Uh, can I just use a bathroom somewhere?"

"Oh!" the woman administrator said, as if she should have known. "Of course you can. Go to where the players went, and there's a bathroom on the right-hand side just before you get to the locker room."

Trevor followed her instructions, walking up a ramp and stepping into the bathroom, where he froze. He could hear the sounds of two men talking and washing their hands at the sinks. Their spikes clattered on the floor, telling him they were players. Trevor heard his name and flattened himself against the wall so they couldn't see him.

"The kid wasn't a bad kid," one player said.

"I know, I know, it's just such a joke, us having to stick around for *that*. I mean, why doesn't the kid just play with other kids? That's one thing that makes me sick about this town. Everybody's kid has to be a star. If you want to be a movie star, be a movie star, okay? Isn't that enough? Now you gotta be a sports star, too? It's just ridiculous."

"Well, the kid's dad is big-time. He was the best man at Mr. McCourt's wedding. That's how it works in this town. I don't hear you complaining about the paycheck."

The players' spiked shoes clacked toward Trevor, and he scooted back outside and down the ramp before turning on his heel and marching up again like it was the first time.

Furcal and Billingsley emerged from the bathroom and waved to him.

"Hey, kid."

"Nice job."

"Yeah, nice job."

Trevor smiled and waved and went into the bathroom, where he hung his head and took deep breaths, trying hard not to throw up.

6

SAM

"I got a kid here looks just like Trevor Goldman," Fuller said into the phone before pausing. "Yes, I do, they're almost identical, and his father's in the business. He's suggesting double time. I offered time and a half. . . . No, you'll have a tough time telling them apart, I promise. It's amazing. Okay, just wanted to make sure it was good with you. It's your budget."

Fuller hung up the phone and offered a false smile. "Double time it is. If you'll be so kind as to finish filling out the required forms, I'll have the contract drawn up before you go."

Sam raised his hand like he was in school. "Mr. Fuller? When do I finish?"

"Finish?"

"Every day. Do they finish at five? And what about weekends?"

Fuller shrugged. "Most times it's nine to five, Monday

through Friday. I can't promise, though. If they get behind, you might have to shoot all night, day and night, seven days a week. It just depends. That's Hollywood. Why?"

"Uh . . ." Sam shifted in his chair. "Dad, can we talk?"

Fuller seemed to think that was funny. He chuckled and got up. "I'll leave you two alone. I'll have my assistant get the paperwork together."

Sam watched Fuller go, then turned to his dad.

"I can't," Sam said.

It was his father's turn to chuckle. "What do you mean, 'can't'?"

"Baseball, remember? I've got league games on Tuesdays *and* the Blue Sox." Sam had gotten over the strange name of his travel team weeks ago. "I've got practice or a game three or four nights a week, and tournaments on the weekends. What if these movie shoots run over? And sometimes we practice during the day, like Friday. Friday we practice in the morning."

"Baseball is a game."

"It's a game I love," Sam said. "It's a game you can make tens of millions of dollars at, hundreds even."

His father laughed out loud.

"That's a long shot, Sam. We've talked about *this*." His father waved a hand around the fancy office and toward the lot outside.

Sam dropped his voice. "A script for a horror film is a long shot, too."

His father scowled. "Hey, this is my life's work. It's my dream, and *Dark Cellar* is the one, Sam."

"What about my dream?" Sam clasped his hands together.

"Coach Sharp says I've got what it takes."

"Coach Sharp." Sam's dad swatted an imaginary fly.

"He played in the pros."

Sam's dad wrinkled his face. "Triple-A."

"But he knows. He says I can make it. Dad, *three weeks* and we'll be in the finals. If I get the MVP, I get an automatic spot in the USC Elite Training Center. Almost *everyone* who goes through that program gets a scholarship. A lot of them make it to the pros. Dad, that's *my* dream. You know all this."

Sam had explained to his father in detail how the University of Southern California—USC—held a tournament for the Los Angeles–area players every year. Besides monster trophies, whoever the USC coaches named as the MVP in the finals got an automatic spot in the USC Elite Training Center, something every kid in the area had heard and dreamed of. Making the finals was no guarantee, but the way the season had gone for Sam's team, it didn't seem like there was anyone around who could stop them.

They were interrupted by a knock at the door. Fuller's assistant marched in and handed a contract to Sam's dad. She smiled and stared at Sam for a minute, obviously impressed with her boss's discovery. After she walked out, Sam's dad studied the contract and licked his lips.

"There's no reason you can't do both. You can miss a Blue Sox practice every once in a while, and the league games don't matter that much. Sam, we could really use this money."

His father waved the contract in the air.

Sam bit his lower lip. "Dad, if I do this, will you promise I can play with my team? Maybe practice I can miss once in a while, but I can't miss a Saturday game, even if they say I have to work. Will you promise?"

Sam's dad got a serious look on his face. "Sam, I've spent my whole life chasing my dream. I'm not going to keep you from yours."

Sam grinned at his father, but in his heart he knew that if push came to shove, the movie business took first place in his father's mind. Baseball was a very distant second. His father laid the contract down on the edge of Fuller's desk and scribbled his signature. Then he handed the pen to Sam.

Sam looked at his father, took a deep breath, and signed on the dotted line.

7

TREVOR

Trevor woke and stared at his ceiling. His mother had hired a famous artist to paint it like the night sky, and he couldn't stop himself from picking out the many constellations he'd learned about from his tutor. He wondered what it would be like to go to school with other kids instead of spending all the boring hours with a tutor on movies sets, at home, or when they traveled to Paris, his mother's favorite place in the world. Trevor sighed and got up. He showered, dressed, and then plugged an iPod into his ears so he could listen to music on his way through the house into the breakfast room. Breakfast was always laid out there on elegant silver service trays on a sideboard.

Trevor took a china plate from the stack and went along the board, picking out crisp bacon, two scoops of scrambled eggs, some tangerine sections, and a blueberry muffin. He carried the plate to the round table nestled into a curve of big bay windows. The view overlooked the terraces that led down to the pool area, complete with its own waterfall. He'd heard people call it beautiful, magnificent, or impressive, but to Trevor the only point of interest were little yellow birds that sometimes hunted insects among the rosebushes.

His mother appeared in a thick silky robe with a turban on her head. She blinked her puffy eyes and took a plate of her own, filling it with berries before sitting down across from Trevor.

"You okay?" he asked.

She yawned and winced and took out her phone to check the messages. "Long night, a charity ball. I can never get away from those things without your father. He's so . . . so . . ."

"Hard-nosed?"

"I was thinking 'urbane.'" His mother turned her attention to the phone.

"Ur-what?"

"It means elegant, dignified," she said without looking up. "'Hard-nosed' isn't so nice."

"It's better than what I was really thinking."

She looked up and smiled at him and they both laughed until she winced again and clutched her forehead.

"Headache?"

"Champagne. It always does that. I'm going back to bed, but I wanted to be a good mother and tell you to have a good day."

Trevor wanted to ask her why she always drank champagne if it felt so bad, but he kept quiet. He also knew his mother well enough that her lapse into total silence for the rest of the meal so she could text didn't offend or upset him. He put his napkin on the plate when he finished and kissed her cheek.

"It's only eight-thirty," she said, looking up. "Is Gabriel getting you early?"

"Thought I'd hit a few."

"You liked that yesterday, right? With the Dodgers?"

"It was amazing," Trevor said. "How many people ever get to do that?"

She squeezed his hand and told him to have a good day, then got back to work on her phone as she climbed the stairs toward her bedroom.

Out front, the limo waited for him with Dolph and Wolf sitting side by side in the front seat. Gabriel sat in back. When the personal assistant saw Trevor, he jumped out of the car and opened the door.

"I told you, you don't have to do that." Trevor walked past the car and headed for the batting cage.

"Taylor Lautner liked when I opened the door." Gabriel caught up to him as he circled the garage.

"I keep telling you, Gabriel, I'm not Taylor Lautner. Why do you always talk about him?"

Gabriel shrugged. "He's the gold standard."

Trevor let himself into the cage, put on a helmet, and picked up a bat. One of the unseen workers had reloaded the machine. All Trevor had to do was step up and hit the balls.

"Do you have to do this?" Gabriel asked.

"Do you have to ask me that every day? The studio is five minutes away."

Gabriel rolled his eyes. Trevor stepped on the footpad that

operated the machine. A yellow rubber baseball came shooting out of the tube with a *thunk*. Trevor swung and hammered the ball past the machine into the netting.

"Nice," he said to himself.

Trevor kept going, pounding pitches until his arms began to ache. It was a good feeling, and it made up for sitting around all day in a dressing room, listening to a tutor, or playing Xbox while he waited for the next scene. Finally, he returned the bat and helmet and left the cage with Gabriel at his side.

"We'll be late now." Gabriel pouted.

Trevor shook his head.

Gabriel pointed to himself. "But I'm the one who gets yelled at by Pierce Everette."

"He doesn't yell, and it always works out. We've both still got jobs, don't we?"

Inside the car, Trevor said hi to Dolph and reached up to scratch Wolf's head before Gabriel handed him his scenes for the day. They rode in silence to the studio, getting out right in front of the enormous soundstage and walking in through a side door. Trevor's eyes had to adjust to the darkness, but in just a few moments, the orange glow of the lava pit provided all the light he needed. The stone walls of the cavern and the dragon sculpture with its missing ruby looked really menacing, even though Trevor could see the wooden framework behind it all. It was a busy set, with people scurrying around, touching up this or that or hammering something into place.

In the middle of the set was his stand-in, well lit and wearing an exact copy of the leather vest and loose white shirt that Trevor would wear for the scene. Trevor stopped for a better look since he knew the old stand-in, Pete, a boy from Santa Monica, had come down with mono and was being replaced. As his eyes continued to adjust, Trevor moved closer. When he saw the new boy's face, he kept moving, right up into the set until they stood face-to-face.

Trevor felt a chill, and when he opened his mouth to speak, his breath was gone. Finally, he held out a hand and said, "I'm Trevor. Nice to meet you."

The other boy looked hard at Trevor. "I'm . . . Sam."

Trevor felt like he was looking in the mirror, and in the back of his mind he wondered if someone was playing some kind of a trick on him. The handshake was over, or it should have been, but for some reason Trevor couldn't let go.

8

SAM

"It's pretty wild," Sam said. "I feel like I'm looking at myself."

Trevor, the movie star, laughed. "I was thinking the exact same thing. I'm glad you've got long hair, or they might not be able to tell us apart. Don't tell me you've got a birthmark under that hair."

Trevor wore his hair buzzed short. He turned his own head and tugged his collar down, showing Sam a raspberry splotch the size of a silver dollar.

"No birthmark," Sam said, using his fingers to raise his hair and expose the back of his own neck as he tucked it into the net they'd given him to keep the hair off his face.

"Man, aside from that, Central Casting is on the ball, right?" Trevor said.

"I guess. Yes."

"Well," Trevor said, "you and I won't get much chance to

hang out because when I'm in there, you're out here and pretty much vice versa. But when we break for lunch, maybe you can come to my dressing room. Do you play Xbox?"

"*Call of Duty*," Sam said. "I like Nazi Zombies."

"Cool. Type your number so I can text you when we're going to play. McKenna Steele plays, too." Trevor handed Sam his phone. "She's hooked on Halo Reach, but she'll play Zombies if you stand your ground."

"McKenna Steele?" Sam punched his number into Trevor's phone.

"She's the costar. Here, I'll send you a blank text so you've got my number, too. In case you need anything."

"I know who she is," Sam said, swallowing because his mouth had gone suddenly dry as his heart skipped a beat. "You play Xbox with her?"

"Her, and you, too, now."

"Oh." Sam jumped when his phone vibrated and he realized it was Trevor's blank message, establishing contact between them.

A tall, thin man with a pinched face and blond hair plastered to his skull appeared and spoke to Trevor. "They want you in makeup and . . . oh!"

The man stared at Sam.

"Oh my God." The man put a hand to his mouth. "Oh my God."

"Gabriel, this is Sam," Trevor said, "the new stand-in. Sam, Gabriel is my assistant. He works for my parents, really. I think they call him my assistant to make me feel better about it. I mean, I'm a little old for a babysitter, right?"

Sam and Trevor grinned at each other.

"I can't believe this," Gabriel said, looking from Sam to Trevor and back again. "Excuse me."

Sam and Trevor watched Gabriel hustle off, pulling a cell phone from his suit coat pocket as he went and dialing someone.

"He's a little overdramatic," Trevor said, "but he's okay. He worked for my dad for years and then spent a couple years with Taylor Lautner, which I'm sure he'll tell you about as soon as he gets the chance."

"Your dad's a big movie producer, right?"

"Yeah, but he's okay. He's in Australia now. Some mega-budget space movie with Russell Crowe. It's a lot bigger than this thing."

"This is pretty impressive." Sam looked around at all the people.

Trevor shrugged. "They're only spending about sixty million."

Sam blinked at the number. "Hey, I know we just met, but my dad's in the business, too."

"He is?"

"Well, kind of. He's a writer. Well, he's an English teacher, but he's a writer, too. He's been writing horror movie scripts for years. He cranks them out like there's no tomorrow."

"Wow," Trevor said. "I love horror. *Chainsaw Massacre, Friday the 13th, Halloween*, the old-school stuff."

"See, that's what my dad's into."

"What's he written? Maybe I saw it."

Sam suddenly felt the heat from the lights. "Well, he hasn't had anything made, yet. That's what I was thinking. I mean, your dad. He might know someone who's looking to do some old-school horror. My dad's got this one right now that people are really interested in, *Dark Cellar*. How good is that name?"

A blank look fell over Trevor's face. "Yeah. Sure. No problem. Well, I gotta get to makeup. See you."

"Yeah, see you." Sam watched him go. He could tell that something he said disturbed Trevor. As soon as he began talking about *Dark Cellar*, everything changed, but Sam had no idea why.

9
SAM

"Don't worry."

Sam spun around to see where the voice had come from.

It was McKenna Steele.

Sam recognized her. She had long dark hair, green eyes, and a small upturned nose. Sam wasn't one to go crazy over girls, but McKenna was beautiful, and even he couldn't help feeling an electric kind of buzz in his stomach.

"Oh, hi," he said, holding out his hand. "I'm Sam. Sam Palomaki. I'm the stand-in."

"I know *what* you are." Her hand was smooth and soft and dry. "Now I know who. Palomaki, that's funny. Not in a bad way. I'm McKenna."

"I know."

"I was down there, studying my lines, and I heard you and Trevor talking. I saw you were confused, so I thought I'd clear it up for you. When you're in this business, you shouldn't ask people for favors about scripts or getting a part for something or other. It always goes through the agents."

"I had no idea," Sam said.

"I know." She spoke lightly, and her face was pleasant. "That's why I'm telling you, not to make you feel bad. Trevor doesn't know what it's like to be a normal kid, but I grew up in Seattle. This whole thing is only a couple years old to me. He was born into it."

Sam glanced in the direction Trevor had disappeared. "I only wanted to help my dad, you know?"

"*I* know," she said. "Don't worry. Just let it be for a while. I thought I heard him ask you to play Xbox, right?"

"Yes."

"Good, when we break for lunch, I'll be there and get everything back to normal. Just don't bring up your dad's script again and it'll all be fine. We'll be here all summer. Who knows, by the end, maybe *I* can bring it up indirectly, and then maybe he'll help."

"You? That's awesome. But you don't even know me."

"I like your face."

Sam blushed.

"Well, I better get to makeup myself," McKenna said. "Good luck."

"I don't really have to do anything."

"I know," she said. "You'll be bored out of your mind, and your back will ache from standing in one spot all day. That's why I say good luck."

"How do you know about the backache?" Sam asked.

McKenna cocked her head at him. "Don't you know? I started out like you. I was a stand-in, then they 'discovered' me. Don't get your hopes up, though. They've already got one of you. Trevor Goldman."

Sam knew by her tone that McKenna wasn't being mean; she was just saying the facts. "I'm a baseball player. I want to play at USC. My team's in USC's big tournament this summer. If we get to the finals like everyone thinks we will, and I win the MVP, I get to go to their Elite Training Center and I'm on my way."

"USC? Wow. That would be hot."

"Then to the pros." Sam spoke almost under his breath, and he looked away. "You know, if I get lucky."

"Maybe you will."

There was a commotion at the entrance to the soundstage. A woman shouted, cursing and barging through a cluster of people until she stood at the bottom of the set, staring up at Sam and McKenna. The woman wore a white robe and a turban and he knew she was someone famous, but Sam couldn't quite say who.

"You!" the woman screamed, pointing at the set so that Sam looked around him at the men working there. "Out!"

A man in a bomber jacket and baseball cap who Sam recognized as the director, Pierce Everette, approached the crazed woman and put two gentle hands on her shoulders. "Diana, please. What's wrong? What are you doing?"

"*Him!* I want him off this set! I want him a million miles away from my son. Don't you ever let him back! Ever! Do you hear me?"

"Diana," the director said calmly. "Who are you talking

40

about? What's the problem?"

The woman trembled, but seemed to gain some composure as she lowered her voice. "Pierce, I'm sorry to barge in here like this, but you know me, and you know my husband, and you know that if I want something, it *will* happen. So please, just remove him from the set. I don't want to go into it. It's not important. I have my reasons. Just make him leave. Now."

Sam's mouth fell open because he realized as all eyes turned his way that the crazy woman was talking about *him*.

10

TREVOR

With the dressing room door open, Trevor could hear his mother's shouting from where he sat. He started to remove the cape and get up out of the makeup chair, then paused, not wanting to get in the way of her anger. He'd done that before and knew it was to be avoided at all costs. While his mother was kind and caring, she could also be equally wicked and vicious. When she was in a rant, his father always said you had to watch out for friendly fire.

When the shouting subsided, Trevor signaled the makeup artist to stop. He swept away the cape and got up, walked along the back of the set, and peeked around into the orange light. His mother spoke in a low tone to the director. Everyone else gave them a wide space. McKenna rounded the corner and almost knocked him down.

"What happened?" he asked her in a hushed voice.

McKenna bit into her lower lip and shook her head. "Nothing. Your mom fired the stand-in."

"Sam?"

McKenna nodded and pointed to the hairnet Sam had dropped on the set.

"Why?"

"You weren't very nice to him, now you care?"

"McKenna, he started asking me about my dad. You know I hate that."

"Helping people?" McKenna made a face.

"People need to help themselves, too."

"People helped me."

"McKenna, I don't mean you."

"I'm just saying, Trevor. He seemed nice and now he just got run off the set. From the way your mom sounded, I doubt he'll get a spot in a crowd scene."

"Well, I didn't say anything to her. I don't even know why she came."

"In her bathrobe."

"Her bathrobe?" Trevor looked out over the set. He now saw Gabriel in the shadows, watching Trevor's mother, but staying clear. "Gabriel."

"Gabriel?"

"He acted really weird when he saw Sam. He freaked out. He must have called her and she came without even bothering to get dressed, but *why*?"

"You two look exactly alike, you know."

"Why would that make him call my mom?"

McKenna looked like she was about to say something.

"What?" Trevor asked.

"No, nothing," she said.

"McKenna, come on."

McKenna hesitated. "He looks *exactly* like you, Trevor. Exactly. And get this: he's really into baseball. Sounds like he's good, too. He's on some team going for the city title this summer. Something about USC scouting him."

"Scouting him for baseball?" Trevor couldn't keep the envy out of his voice.

"That's what he said."

"You think Sam and I are related or something?"

"Trevor . . . what if you and Sam are twins?"

11

TREVOR

Trevor grabbed McKenna by the arm and dragged her back into his dressing room, closing the door behind them and locking it.

"What are you talking about?" Trevor felt a knot in his stomach. He backed up, feeling for a stool to sit down on. "How?"

"Well, you were adopted, right?"

The knot turned into a wave of nausea. Trevor was adopted. He'd known about it ever since he could remember, but he and his parents never discussed it. It was like the knowledge that he had a grandfather who had committed suicide: He knew it, they knew it, everyone knew it, but no one mentioned it because it didn't seem polite.

McKenna just waited.

"Yes," he said under his breath.

"Well? Why couldn't there have been two of you?"

McKenna wrinkled her face. "I don't mean two of *you*. That didn't come out right. I just mean, twins. Why couldn't that be possible?"

"Because, don't you think I would have known? Don't you think they would have told me that? Isn't that something pretty important? Something special?" Trevor clenched his hands. "Who would do that?"

"Relax," McKenna said. "Maybe they didn't know."

"Or maybe that's why Gabriel freaked when he saw Trevor. Maybe *he* knew. He was working for my father back then. Maybe they all know, and he called my mom and she raced down here in her bathrobe because they don't want me to figure this out."

McKenna stared at him. "What are you going to do?"

Trevor thought, then said, "Nothing. I'm going to play stupid. If my mom doesn't want me to know, I'll pretend I don't."

"But then what are you going to do?" McKenna asked.

"Then? Then, I'm going to find him."

12

SAM

Sam sat in Donald Fuller's office, staring at the carpet. The door opened and his father spilled into the room.

"What happened? What did you do?"

"I didn't do anything," Sam said.

Sam's father rarely got mad, but when he did, his nose turned red. "You don't just do nothing and end up getting thrown off a set."

The door opened again and Fuller sat down behind his desk, making a steeple with his fingertips and planting it beneath his chin.

"I'd like to know, too," Fuller said. "This whole thing is a mess."

Sam shook his head. "The only thing I did was talk to Trevor Goldman and I mentioned *Dark Cellar*. When I asked him if he could maybe get his dad to look at it, he got kind of weird, but it wasn't a big deal."

"*Dark Cellar*?" Fuller rumpled his brow.

"My script." Sam's dad spoke softly.

Fuller slapped a hand flat on his polished desk. "That's it. Why in the world would you bother Trevor Goldman? You're the stand-in. You stand there and say nothing. Didn't anyone tell you that?"

"They told me, but *he* started talking to *me*."

"What, to ask you to step aside?" Fuller said, knitting his brows. "You broke the cardinal rule. You're a stand-in. You don't bother the star. Now it all makes sense. Well, at least I don't feel so bad about you two being blackballed from the studio. I mean, I'm sorry, but I'm not that sorry. We can't have extras and stand-ins taking advantage of their contact with the stars."

"Blackballed?" Sam's dad muttered the word and stared at his own hands.

"I didn't take advantage," Sam said, growing angry himself. "He asked me to play Xbox. He gave me his cell number to text him!"

Sam held up his phone.

"Give me that phone." Fuller's voice grew heated. "You can't have his cell number."

"I do have it. He gave it to me."

"Let me see." Fuller snapped his fingers and held out a hand.

"No." Sam stuffed the phone back in his pocket.

Fuller pointed a finger at him. "If you know what's good for you, you'll never use it. You'll get rid of it. You and your dad are blackballed from Paramount, but if this gets nasty, Gerry

Goldman is not a guy you want out there saying bad things about you. You could be blackballed across this entire town. Cut your losses, kid. Nice try, but that's not how the business works. That's what agents are for."

"Blackballed?" Sam's dad spoke louder this time and looked like someone had doused him with cold water. "I've got a deal pending on my *Dark Cellar* script. So far, they love it. I'm waiting for an option deal and it looks like a green light is just around the corner. That's how we ended up here in the first place. I can't be blackballed."

"You are." Fuller stood up. "Neither of you are allowed onto the Paramount lot again. They asked me to escort you out."

"I'm not going," Sam's dad said. "I've got a deal pending. This guy gets it. He believes in this script. We're going to get a *deal* any day now. Any day."

"Come on. Don't make me call security," Fuller said. "Don't make this ugly."

"It already is ugly. My son didn't do anything wrong. You people are crazy."

"You said you're in the business." Fuller spoke more quietly now, reasoning with Sam's dad. "You know how it goes. You can't harass one of the stars on a set. It's fatal. You know that."

Sam felt sick when his father dropped his head and stood up to go. "I know. Come on, Sam."

"Dad, this isn't fair. I'm telling you."

"I know. That's life, Son. Things are never fair. Let's go."

Fuller admired the Ferrari as they climbed inside, and he had the decency to wish them luck. Sam kept quiet, resting his head against the car window as they left the cool blue shade of the palm trees in Hollywood for the waffling heat of a million cars and a billion homes sweltering under a brown sky, heavy with smog.

Sam could smell the landfill well before it appeared like a giant dung heap, swirling with seagulls instead of flies. Sam's dad settled the Ferrari into its spot and cut the engine. He put his hands on the wheel and sighed.

That's when Sam's phone buzzed.

He took it from his pocket, expecting the text to be from one of his teammates but finding something completely different.

"Dad," he said, his voice brimming with excitement, "it's a text . . . it's from Trevor Goldman."

13

TREVOR

Trevor's phone buzzed. He read Sam's reply and showed it to McKenna.

"Can you do that?" McKenna asked.

"Watch me," Trevor said.

The stage manager knocked on the door. He apologized to Trevor for the delay, saying they had some technical issues with the lighting but that they were ready for him now. Trevor opened the door, and McKenna followed him out onto the set. Gabriel appeared, trying not to look flustered.

"Who was yelling out here?" Trevor asked him. "I thought I heard shouting."

"Something about the stand-in," Gabriel said. "There were some issues. Anyway, they got another one."

"Issues?" Trevor admired the way Gabriel hid the truth without actually lying.

51

"You should ask Pierce."

They both knew that Trevor wouldn't ask the director such a thing when they were ready for a shot. Pierce was famous for his intense focus and his equally intense displeasure when someone distracted him. The closer he got to the shot, the angrier he was if someone disturbed him.

"No big deal," Trevor said, noting the relief on Gabriel's face.

Trevor stepped up onto the set and watched the new stand-in disappear. He was surprised at how quickly they'd managed to produce another boy with nearly the same size, shape, and hair color as Trevor and Sam, but they did it. Trevor took his mark. Someone handed him a sword.

"Okay, Trevor, remember what's just happened." The director's voice came from behind the bright lights. "Your mother's been killed and you're crushed. I want you fighting back the tears. Then, *boom*, out of the lava, the living dragon appears, and you're stunned because now you know the legend she always told you is true. You got it?"

"I got it," Trevor said, conjuring up the emotions that Pierce Everette was asking for.

"Okay, now I'll cue you on the dragon. We'll CG that in, but I want you to be shocked, completely in awe."

"Got it," Trevor said, breathing deep and putting himself into a kind of trance.

"And . . . action!"

Trevor gave the director what he wanted . . . almost. They did twelve takes before Pierce called it quits and Trevor got to go back to his dressing room. McKenna headed onto the set as he was leaving and slapped him a high five like they were tag team wrestlers, one going off while the other took over the battle.

Back in the dressing room, Trevor dialed up his mom. He heard the caution in her voice as she greeted him, but he pretended not to notice. "Can I go to McKenna's to swim and have a cookout after we're done shooting? I guess she's gonna have some people over."

"I've got a dinner with the hospital board anyway, so that works out great. Sure. I'll be done about nine-thirty; can I pick you up then on my way home?"

"Great. Thanks, Mom."

"Everything else okay?"

"Sure. Like what?"

"I don't know . . . anybody unusual you meet today?"

Trevor pretended to think. "No, Everette had his family here yesterday, some cousins or something I took pictures with. That who you mean?"

His mom hesitated. "Yes, them. I'm glad you met them. Everette doesn't have a lot of family. Have fun, angel."

Trevor got off and smiled to himself.

14
SAM

Sam's dad spent the rest of the day writing while Sam dug deeper into *The Count of Monte Cristo*. When his dad finally left his desk and stretched his back, he asked Sam if he wanted to go get something to eat before being dropped off at McKenna Steele's.

"I think we're having dinner there. I'm ready when you are."

Sam's dad pushed the curtain aside and studied the Ferrari. "Let me just wash down the car. It won't take thirty or forty minutes."

Sam knew better than to argue. If his dad was driving into the heart of Beverly Hills, he was going in a clean Ferrari. He returned to his bedroom and picked up his book. Forty-five minutes later, Sam heard a shout from out front. The Ferrari shone like a polished gem and his dad beamed with pride.

"Nice," Sam said.

They climbed in and headed toward town in style. The Ferrari was on its best behavior, and Sam's dad clucked his tongue as they turned up McKenna's street.

"McKenna Steele." Sam's dad touched his own forehead. "I can't believe it."

"I told you, Dad, she's just a nice person. We hit it off." Sam stared out the window at the beautiful homes packed together along Beverly Drive.

"In five minutes?" Sam's father sat up straight and stuck his arm out of the window, obviously proud of their ride.

"She said she liked my face. This is it, twenty-seven-nineteen." Sam pointed to the number on the stone gatepost of a Spanish-style yellow home with a red clay tile roof and wrought-iron balconies that matched the front gate.

Sam's dad eased the car up into the circular stone driveway. Sam hopped out and headed for the front door.

"Well, have fun," his dad said through the open window. "I'll pick you up at eight-thirty."

Sam turned and waved to him, wishing his father would stop sitting in his car gawking at the house. Sam rang the bell. A maid with a strange accent greeted him warmly and said McKenna was out back at the pool. Sam turned and gave his father one last wave. His father's face beamed with pride, as if Sam had just hit a grand-slam home run in a championship game. Sam had his swimsuit in a plastic grocery bag and he held it up, asking the maid if there was a place he could change.

She told him there was a pool house and led him through

a home with towering ceilings and plaster walls covered with fancy oil paintings in thick gold frames of carved wood. Antique furniture sat on large Oriental rugs. Sam tried not to touch anything.

Out in back, carefully sculpted shrubs and trees surrounded a rectangular pool and a small cottage with a roof that matched the big house's. At the end by the diving board, McKenna and Trevor sat on thick lounge chairs, both intent on their own iPhones.

The maid pointed out the pool house to Sam, saying he could change there and asking if he would like a drink.

"Gatorade would be great, if you have it," Sam said, waving to the movie stars as he slowly descended the wide stone steps.

After changing, Sam studied his muscles in the mirror, clenching his hands and looking for veins in his forearms before he moved up to his teeth and scowled at the uneven edges of his two top fronts. After looking at himself in the mirror for too long, Sam emerged from the pool house with a towel around his shoulders and sat down in a chair next to Trevor.

"Glad you could make it." Trevor slapped Sam a high five.

"You've got some house." Sam looked at McKenna.

McKenna put her iPhone aside. "Thanks. Glad you could make it."

The maid brought drinks for them all. Sam sipped at his and watched the other two to see what he should do. They put their drinks on one of the cocktail tables and Sam did the same.

"We asked you here for a reason," Trevor said.

"He's always planning things," McKenna said.

"It stinks what happened." Trevor's face looked sorry, but

Sam couldn't help remembering that he was an actor. Then Trevor said, "Do you think we could be twins?"

Sam felt like someone had punched him in the face. He blinked. "What?"

Trevor shrugged. "Come on. Look at us. McKenna?"

"You're pretty exact."

Trevor swung his legs off the lounge chair so that he sat sideways and closer to Sam. "You're adopted, right?"

"How did you know?"

"If we're twins, that's what happened. Your birthday was yesterday, right?"

"No," Sam said, actually feeling some relief. "My birthday is *July* second, not June."

Trevor looked at McKenna with confusion. McKenna sat sideways on her chair now, too, and said, "What if someone just changed the month on the birth certificate. How hard would that be? It's just two letters."

"I'm not from here," Sam said. "I'm from Sandusky, Ohio."

Trevor waved a hand through the air. "We could have been born in Tibet. That doesn't matter. Look, I think it's why my mom freaked out."

"It wasn't about me asking you to help with my dad's script?" Sam asked.

"I told you that when we texted." Trevor held up his phone as a reminder. "We think she doesn't want me to know about you, and the fact that I have a brother out there."

"Why would she care?" Sam asked.

Trevor shrugged. "I don't want to sound snooty, but people like my mom think different. They always worry that people

57

want things from them. Or, maybe she feels guilty? Maybe she knew about both of us and chose me. You got left behind."

"I'm not 'left behind,'" Sam said. "My dad's the greatest."

"I didn't mean that."

"Okay."

"You're a good baseball player, right?"

"I'm good. Yeah."

"On some big travel team? Playing for a city title?"

"With the chance to get into USC's Elite Training Center."

Trevor nodded vigorously. "All right. So, I've got something that's going to sound crazy, but I want you to think about it. I want you to think about how great it would be for you and for me."

Sam squinted at Trevor. The fancy house and pool and the maid and pool house, along with the eager look on McKenna's face, made him feel like a fly in a spider's web.

"What would?" Sam asked.

"I want us, you and me . . . to trade places."

15

TREVOR

"For how long?" Sam asked.

Trevor was surprised at Sam's question, but maybe he shouldn't have been. If they really were twins—and Trevor had no doubt now that they were—then it made sense that they'd think alike, too.

"I don't know how long. A couple weeks? Not forever." Trevor laughed at that idea.

Sam nodded, thinking. "Why?"

"You can live the life of a movie star." Trevor opened his hands and held them out to Sam as if to give it all to him right then and there. "You want to go to the beach and have a campfire? You fly in a helicopter to Malibu. You want to have a party? We've got a video arcade, a soda fountain, a home theater, a bunk room, pool, guesthouse, bowling alley, dance floor, three-hole golf course, almost anything you can think of."

"No," Sam said, cutting him off. "I'm not asking why for me. I'm asking why for you?"

Trevor laughed. "Baseball. I want to *play*."

"Why can't you play?"

Trevor felt his face scrunch up. "Why can't I? I know. It's crazy, but my mom says no. My career is the reason. My career and my parents' lifestyle. When I'm not in a movie, we're off living in Paris or Tahiti or someplace nuts on location with my dad, or with my mom. Travel team baseball doesn't have a place in my world. Man, I don't even go to *school*."

Trevor almost said "It stinks," but he kept his wits about him and held his tongue. He wanted this trade, so he didn't want Sam thinking his life was anything but a fun-filled adventure on Easy Street.

"How are you gonna play for me?" Sam asked. "I play all the time. I'm good. I'm real good. My team's gotta make it into the finals for me to get to USC."

"I can carry your weight. I don't play, but I bet I practice as much as you, if not more. Every chance I get. I've got my own batting cage. I've got a coach who comes three times a week. You know who Tom Royal is? He used to play for the Dodgers. He says I've got what it takes. My dad laughs and says he's trying to sell me more private lessons, but I know I'm good. I could do it. I just need the chance."

Sam went quiet. He looked down at his bare feet. "I live by a landfill."

"I don't care," Trevor said, the excitement building in him.

"Listen to this, this is why, no matter what else, I *know* you'll want to do it."

Trevor allowed a dramatic pause, the way he would if he was delivering a big line in a movie.

"You can get your dad's script into the right people's hands."

"The right people?"

"Producers, agents, directors, studio executives," Trevor said. "When you're me, you're going to have access to everyone, and if you say you want them to do it, if you say you want to act in it? Then you can get your father's movie to get optioned and then all the way to a *green light*."

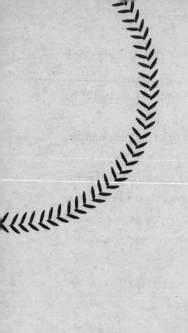

16
SAM

Sam's eyes lost focus for a moment. Trevor flashed a grin at McKenna.

She clapped her hands. "This is like something in a movie, only it's real."

"Won't people know?" Sam asked.

"Not if we cut your hair. McKenna's got some tanning spray and a way to give you a birthmark like mine. No one will ever know, and if either of us has questions or problems? We'll just text each other."

"How is she going to give me a birthmark?"

"A Sharpie."

Sam wrinkled his nose. "Like, a Magic Marker?"

"Just trust me. We tested it. Look."

Trevor turned his neck so Sam could see the dots right next to his birthmark made by a Sharpie marker.

"What about my hair?" Sam asked. "People are going to ask why I all of a sudden look like you."

"I bet they won't," McKenna said.

Sam gave her a puzzled look.

"Listen, think about any picture you've ever seen of Trevor, any movie he's been in," McKenna said.

"Why?" Sam asked.

"His hair. He's never had his hair short like this before. The only people who've seen him are the people on the set and his closest friends and family. Your dad, the guys on your baseball team, anyone you know won't think your hair looks like Trevor's, and *Dragon's Empire* won't be in theaters for over a year."

"She's right." Trevor ran a hand over his scalp. "People are going to notice you cut your hair, but they're not going to say, 'Oh, that looks like Trevor Goldman.' None of them have seen me like this in the movies."

"What about your mom?" Sam asked.

Trevor shrugged. "I love my mom, but she doesn't pay that close attention. I usually don't see her outside of breakfast, and she's usually got a headache. My dad might pick up on it, but he's in Australia for the next three weeks."

"My dad will know," Sam said. "He'll ask about the hair. He'll *know* you're not me. I'm with him all the time."

"Let me ask you something," Trevor said. "What kind of a guy is your dad?"

"What do you mean?"

"Nice guy? Mean? Easygoing? A hard nose? What's he like?"

"He's nice," Sam said. "Kind of easygoing. He's smart."

"Give me a shot at him," Trevor said. "I'm an actor, and I'm not bad, right, McKenna?"

McKenna nodded.

"Let me see if I can't convince him that I'm you and that you asked McKenna to buzz your hair because it's in style. I can lighten my skin with some makeup and cover the birthmark. I'll give it a shot. And if it doesn't work? That's when I tell him about the script. You think he'll play along if we get his script into the hands of the top producers and agents in Hollywood?"

Sam looked around at the beautiful pool, the gardens, the clean-cut hedges, all of it painted in golden sunlight. He knew it was how his dad wanted to live, his dream, what he worked so hard for every day. Sam stared at Trevor for a moment, then nodded his head. "Yes. I do."

"Okay, McKenna," Trevor said, "get the clippers."

17

TREVOR

Sam's eyes shifted nervously as Trevor buzzed up one side of his head and down the other. He sat on a bar stool they'd brought out onto the garden path. His long blond hair fell away in sheets.

McKenna, who now wore an oversized T-shirt over her suit, held some up and giggled. "Aw, I liked the long hair."

Trevor thought Sam looked like he might throw up. When Trevor was done, Sam ran his hand over the stubble and winced.

"It'll be worth it," Trevor said. "The chance of a lifetime."

McKenna clapped.

Trevor and Sam traded clothes, then the three of them ate dinner. A woman McKenna said was the cook served them out on the terrace above the pool—filet mignon grilled with vegetables. She gave Trevor and Sam funny looks, but said nothing. Trevor insisted they swap as many stories about each other's lives as they could, from the boring everyday routines to the more fabulous events, like when Trevor met the Dalai Lama or when Sam's father won a baseball mitt signed by Sandy Koufax at a Hollywood charity fundraiser that he'd emptied his savings account to attend.

"Let me ask you something," Trevor said. "What bothers you about your dad?"

Sam shrugged. "Nothing, really."

"I don't mean anything bad. Is there something you nag him about? Something he does that you can't stand?"

"I guess I'm always trying to get him to eat," Sam said. "He's pretty skinny and his mind is working all the time, and I think sometimes he just forgets to eat."

"Good," Trevor said. "Where?"

"Where to eat? I don't know. Anywhere."

"Where do you like to go?" Trevor asked.

"In and Out Burger, all the way."

"Chocolate shake? Well-done fries?"

"How'd you know?" Sam asked.

"A hunch."

While Sam wanted to know about the routine of a star on the set, Trevor couldn't get enough about baseball and Sam's team, the Blue Sox.

That's how Trevor found out about Dorian Klum.

"He's a big lug is what he is," Sam said through his food. "But he's a good player. Don't pay any attention to him. He likes to give me grief, me and everyone else, especially when you make a mistake."

"The coaches don't stop him?" Trevor asked, already thinking of the business he'd like to give to Klum.

"He's pretty sneaky about it." Sam stabbed the last piece of his steak, stuffed it into his mouth, and chewed.

"And, you said the USC Elite thing is between you and him?" Trevor asked.

"That's what everyone thinks. Klum and I are the best players on the team."

"You're that good?" Trevor couldn't help admiring his twin.

Sam swallowed his food. "Better than Klum, too, but not by much. That's why we've got to make the switch before the finals. I've got to be the one those USC scouts see."

"I told you. I'm good." Trevor made a fist and thumped his chest.

"Even if you are, I can't take the chance. USC is everything to me."

"Don't worry," Trevor said. "I get it. I wouldn't do that to you, and I won't forget what you're doing for me, I promise."

"Me, too." Sam drank some Gatorade from his glass and rattled the ice. "If *Dark Cellar* gets made? I'll be having you guys over for dinner by *my* pool."

"It's a deal," Trevor said.

Sam gave him a quizzical look and Trevor realized he was staring. "Sorry, it's just that I can't get over it. You know how they say that when you die you float outside yourself? It's like I'm afraid I'm dying and I'm seeing myself before I go."

"No," McKenna said, punching Trevor's shoulder, "you're still here. Let's put on the finishing touches. I can still tell you two apart pretty easily."

McKenna led them upstairs to her room. Trevor saw Sam's

eyes go wide at the sight of the room that looked like it belonged to a fairy-tale princess. In its center on a raised platform sat a huge four-poster bed with a red silk canopy. McKenna pulled out the chair at her dressing table by the window and looked at Trevor.

"You first."

Trevor let McKenna apply dabs of makeup, rubbing it in with a soft pad before stepping back, then dusting him with some powder. She covered Trevor's birthmark completely, then blended the makeup in with the rest of his neck.

Trevor looked at his face in the mirror, then up at Sam, who stood over his shoulder. "Wow."

"Here, I'll give you this makeup so you can do it yourself after you take a shower. Put it in your pocket, and don't forget."

"I won't." Trevor stuffed the two round, flat containers in his pocket.

"Okay, Sam," McKenna said, "your turn."

Trevor got up and watched McKenna transform Sam with some long-lasting tanning spray. When his skin tone was dark enough, she moved to his neck. She took out a purple Sharpie marker and removed the cap before dabbing at the base of Sam's skull to re-create Trevor's birthmark just below the hairline in back. She worked slowly and carefully, then stepped back.

"You did it," Trevor said.

McKenna looked back and forth at them. "Yeah. I did. It'll last a few days at a time, and I can keep touching it up at the studio."

"It's scary." Sam peered hard into the mirror.

Suddenly the phone on the dressing table blinked and beeped

and a voice came over the intercom. "McKenna? Your friend's father is here."

Trevor looked at his watch—just after eight. "He's early."

"That's my dad." Sam stood up.

The three of them walked downstairs. When the maid saw them, her eyes went wide and she put a hand to her open mouth before walking away shaking her head and muttering to herself in some foreign language.

"Will she tell?" Sam asked.

McKenna watched her go and giggled. "Not a peep, neither will the cook. That's why my parents love them. They won't say anything about anything. My parents don't know that it works for me, too."

Trevor shook Sam's hand. "Good luck."

"Are you sure?" Sam's face was heavy with worry. "I mean, this all seems so crazy."

"Think of all the good things." Trevor didn't want to turn back now. Not only was he hungry to play in a real baseball game with a bunch of really talented kids, he loved the thrill of the ruse, and the challenge. And, he couldn't think of anything bad that could come from it, even if they got caught. "Think of *Dark Cellar* and your own swimming pool."

Sam nodded, and McKenna patted him on the back.

"Remember, text me if you have questions, and I'll do the same." Trevor took out his phone, handing it to Sam before holding out his hand for the trade.

"What do I do when I get a text?" Sam asked.

"Don't worry. Sometimes I answer people, sometimes I don't," Trevor said. "No one will know but McKenna. If it looks like an emergency from someone else, just forward it to me. Okay, McKenna. Here I go."

Trevor let himself out of the front door, jogged down the steps, and let himself into the passenger seat.

"So, how was—" Sam's dad stopped talking. His mouth fell open, his eyes widened, and he leaned toward Trevor. He blinked, then his face turned dark.

"Is this supposed to be a joke? Where is Sam?"

Trevor took a deep breath.

18
TREVOR

Trevor ran a hand over his buzzed scalp, even though the novelty had worn off for him months ago when he'd first cut it. "Dad, it's me. I cut my hair."

Sam's dad sat, stunned, then narrowed his eyes. "Cut your hair? Why?"

Trevor shrugged and put on an embarrassed face. "McKenna said it's the style. That's how Trevor Goldman wears his."

"You're not Trevor Goldman."

"You don't like it?"

Sam's father's face softened a bit. He spoke softly. "Sam, I love you for you. You don't need style. You don't need to look like a movie star. It's scary how much you do, though. Look like Trevor Goldman, I mean."

"We had filet mignon grilled on the barbecue," Trevor said,

71

remembering Sam's face when he first saw their dinner and knowing that if it had impressed Sam, it would impress his dad and throw him off.

"Really? What else happened?"

Trevor was relieved when Sam's dad put the car into gear and pulled out of the driveway. Trevor added some excitement to his voice and began to describe the pool, the gardens, the cook, and the maid.

"Wow," Sam's dad said. "Nice."

"Speaking of food." Trevor pointed to an In and Out Burger place at the corner ahead. "How about we stop and you get something to eat. Did you eat?"

Sam's dad rubbed the back of his neck. "No, I forgot."

"Dad."

"I know. I know. But you already ate."

"I can always go for a chocolate shake. You know that."

"'He hath eaten me out of house and home; he hath put all my substance into that fat belly of his.'" Sam's dad gave Trevor a questioning look. "Well?"

"Well, what?" Trevor asked, afraid he was blowing it, but able to think of nothing else.

Sam's dad sighed. "Come on, you can't say I haven't used this one on you before. Henry the Fourth, remember?"

"Sure. Oh yeah." Trevor realized Sam's father had given him a quote from Shakespeare. At least the next time, he'd know to guess *Othello* or something.

Sam's dad didn't seem upset, though. He patted Trevor on the shoulder and smiled. Trevor felt a warm glow inside him.

The toughest part was over. All he had to do was hang in there until tomorrow morning and he'd be practicing baseball at a real practice with a real team, getting ready for a real game coming up on Saturday.

19

SAM

Sam watched the car disappear down McKenna's street. He let the curtain fall back into place.

"Well, he must have done it." McKenna grinned.

"So far," Sam said, rubbing bristles on the top of his head.

"It won't get any tougher than the shock of seeing you with that haircut."

"You don't know my dad," Sam said.

"You don't know Trevor. He said he's not bad as an actor, but that's not true. He's not just 'not bad,' he's excellent. He'll *be* you. I've seen him do it. It's pretty amazing."

McKenna led Sam back through the house and outside to the pool, where they sat down in the lounge chairs. Even though the summer sun had dropped behind the trees, lowering the temperature, it was still quite light out.

Sam chuckled, feeling a bit uncomfortable. "He can't just *be* me."

McKenna's face was serious. "He can. Really. Did you see him listening to you when you told him about your life? Did you watch his eyes, studying you like that, not only what you said but how you said it? It's like he can open his brain and suck in who you are."

"You like him a lot."

McKenna studied him, then put a finger under her chin and tilted her head. "Not like you think."

"What do I think?"

"Like a boyfriend. Not like that. He's great, though. Nice. Smart."

Sam let his head hang, and he ran a finger along the lines of his other palm. "If he can be me, you think I can be him?"

"I don't think you should." McKenna gently poked his shoulder. "I think you should be you."

Sam felt his face catch fire. When he looked at her, she didn't blink but only smiled, and it seemed to him like a dream. He couldn't speak.

"Come on." McKenna got up and walked over to a hot tub sunken into the garden at the other end of the pool.

"Can I?" Sam looked at his newly tanned arms.

"It's waterproof," she said. "The Sharpie, too. Both should last three or four days easy."

McKenna turned the bubbles on and slipped in with her T-shirt still on, then tilted her head back, looking up at the sky. "I like the clouds, and the way the sky is so many different colors of blue and then sometimes yellow and pink, purple, even green. Do you ever look at the sky?"

"Most of the time where I live it's pretty brown." Sam slipped into the tub and tilted his head back too, surprised at how pretty it really was, the high horse-tail wisps of white cloud turning yellow, and the blue like a robin's egg.

After a couple minutes, Sam asked, "When do I go home? To Trevor's house, I mean?"

McKenna rolled her head over to look at him. "Bet you can't wait to see it."

"I guess. I'm more worried about his mom than I am excited about seeing the house. I don't know if I'm going to be having too much fun."

"Oh no." McKenna sat up. "You've got to have fun. That's what this whole thing is. It's about fun. It's a story. I said that. It's a real story. Sam's mom won't notice. She'll be on her phone, that you can bet on."

"Her phone?"

"The woman is either texting or talking twenty-four seven. Except when she sleeps. I've seen her texting in the bathroom. Yeah, don't shake your head."

"I'm sure she looks at him."

"Maybe a glance here and there," McKenna said. "I don't think she listens much, even if she looks. You'll be fine."

"That sounds lonely," Sam said.

"It's just his mom. She's a workaholic."

"He said he doesn't even go to school."

"Trevor has people around him all the time. Everyone loves

him. Everyone wants him. It's fun."

Sam shifted in his seat, the bathing suit suddenly feeling wound up and tight from the bubbles. He tugged the legs back down to his knees. "I think I'm getting waterlogged."

"Let's get out. We can play Xbox until she gets here."

"Sounds good."

Sam dried off and changed into Trevor's clothes in the pool house. When he came out, McKenna had on a robe. She led him inside to a small TV room with a leather couch and bookshelves on either side of the TV. McKenna opened a wood panel beneath the screen and took out two controllers.

"Most girls don't play Xbox," Sam said, feeling silly at the sound of his own words.

"I'm not most girls, right?" McKenna winked at him.

Sam's face burned again.

"Nazi Zombies?"

"Halo?"

"How about something in between?" She laughed and sat down, and they logged into a game of Left4Dead2. They fought side by side, reviving each other, sharing health packs, and laughing out loud.

Sam was surprised when his phone buzzed and the text was from Trevor's mom.

I'm here :)

Sam looked at McKenna. "She's here."

McKenna put down her controller and stood up. "You okay?"

"No. I'm not a great actor. I'm not even an actor. I'm a base-ball player."

McKenna led Sam to the front door. "I think you should pretend you don't feel well. That's even if she notices you."

"Is she really that bad?"

"She's not bad. She's a movie star. You'll like her. I do. But she's got a lot going on."

Sam looked at the doorknob. He reached for it, but his hand trembled. There was a mirror on the wall beside a grandfather clock. Sam peered into it.

"You're sure this can work?"

"I'm not sure of anything." McKenna's eyes seemed to sparkle. "That's what makes it fun. Don't worry. Nothing *bad* can happen."

Sam nodded, and McKenna swung the door open for him. She kissed Sam on the cheek, and he seemed to float down the steps and across the walkway to the big rumbling blue car. He opened the car door and smelled leather. He slid into the seat, clutching Trevor's phone.

Trevor's mom put her own phone down and looked over at him. "Oh, angel, look at you. Don't you feel well?"

20

SAM

Too afraid to talk, Sam clutched his stomach and shook his head.

"Like you're going to throw up?"

Sam nodded.

"Well, roll the window down if you do. Maybe roll it down anyway, just in case. The air might help make you better."

Trevor's mom circled the driveway and headed out into the street. Sam glanced at her once, stunned by how pretty she was, even though he already knew what she looked like from the movies. McKenna was right about her, though, because she was already at work texting on her phone and paying no attention to him at all. Sam breathed a little easier, and by the time they pulled through the gates of the Bel Air mansion, he felt like the whole thing really might play out okay.

Trevor's mom stopped at the front entrance, where wide marble stairs rose up toward columns that reminded Sam of a Greek temple. The house seemed to go on forever in both directions, disappearing behind towering trees before he could see its end. Trevor's mom left the car's engine running as they got out. She was busy talking on her phone and Sam wondered if she had simply forgotten to turn it off, but when he glanced back over his shoulder from the top of the steps, he saw a man in a dark suit appear from nowhere, get into the car, and drive off.

Another man in a suit stood just inside the entrance wearing a calm look on his face. Softly he asked, "Is there anything you'll be needing, madam?"

Trevor's mom waved the butler away without stopping her phone conversation and began to climb the wide spiral stairs, evidently forgetting all about her son being sick. The towering white statue of some naked guy in the entryway took Sam's breath away. The statue's stern eye seemed fixed on Sam.

"And you, Master Trevor?" The butler was completely unruffled by the mother's treatment. He spoke with an English accent, as if hot food filled his mouth.

"Oh. Me? What?"

The butler gave Sam a funny look, then cleared his throat. "Is there anything you need?"

Sam didn't know what to say. Trevor hadn't mentioned a butler. Sam wondered what his name was and how Trevor would normally treat the man. "No, no. I'm fine."

"Not a chocolate shake?"

Sam started to say yes, then remembered he was supposed

to be sick. He clutched his stomach and shook his head. "Not feeling too well."

"I see."

Sam felt the butler's eyes on him as he climbed the stairs. Sam knew from Trevor to go to the top of the stairs, then take a left and go all the way to the end, take another left, and his bedroom was the first door on the right.

"Left, left, right." Sam whispered to himself as he looked around, trying to keep his feet moving instead of stopping to stare at the rich surroundings of dark, shiny wood, polished marble, glimmering crystal, heavy curtains, and thick rugs. One painting made him freeze, though. It was Trevor's mom and dad. The painting filled the landing wall on a second stairway. It stood at least twelve feet high. Trevor's father wore a dark suit with a bloodred tie. His silver hair seemed to flow back from his face as if he'd been looking into the mouth of a coming storm. His dark eyes scowled under a thick brow and seemed to be fully charged with death rays.

Sam swallowed and kept going. He finally arrived, and knew it was Trevor's room because the ceiling looked like outer space. He stepped slowly across the threshold, marveling at the huge flat-screen TV, the giant Mac computer screen at the desk, and the movie posters with Trevor's face on them.

Sam fished through the drawers and poked around the closet, amazed at the sports jerseys signed by people like Sammy Sosa, Peyton Manning, Shaquille O'Neal, and Drew Brees. Apparently Trevor *wore* the jerseys instead of framing them for the wall. Sam looked around, feeling almost guilty, then saw there were actually *two* signed by Nolan Ryan, so he pulled one over his head. He took a deep breath and spotted a baseball mitt on a shelf by the window. Sam put it on. It fit perfectly, but it needed more breaking in. While his own glove responded to the slightest flex of his fingers, this one moved a bit stiffly. He flexed his hand, thinking about the batting cage and wondering if he could try it out.

He couldn't remember if Trevor said he used it at night. He didn't recall Trevor saying he had a bedtime, either. Sam's father made him go to bed at ten every night. If Sam wanted to read until eleven he could, but once eleven came around, it was lights out. Sam pushed open two glass doors and stepped out onto a terrace. Little white flowers hung from the green vines that crept up the side of the house. Sam moved his face closer to the flowers and inhaled a scent so sweet it nearly lifted him off his feet. He looked out through the trees and across the lawn and saw the golf course Trevor spoke about, lit by spotlights in the bushes, glowing green even in the night. Beyond the course and the treetops, Sam could see the huddled shapes of the hills and the twinkling lights of the other nearby mansions tucked into their flanks like gems. He suddenly felt very alone and frightened.

He had no business being here and he knew it. Sam took off the Nolan Ryan jersey and laid it on the bed. He tugged Trevor's phone from his pocket and sent a text to his own phone.

i cant do this. we got 2 switch bk

Sam paced the room, waiting for Trevor's reply.
Finally, the phone buzzed.

21
TREVOR

Trevor lay in bed with the light on, pretending to read Sam's book, *The Count of Monte Cristo*. He was too excited to really read. He loved it—his tiny room at the end of a short hall, the cramped bathroom. Trevor smelled only the hint of garbage beneath Sam's father's apple pipe smoke. It was all so real, so rough. It made Trevor's existence seem as fake as a movie set.

And Sam's dad? The man was a hoot, a character you just couldn't make up, with his snippets of Shakespeare, the click of his keyboard, and that delicious smoke snaking its way up from the doorway of his little office to crawl along the ceiling. Trevor looked at the baseball trophies glimmering down at him from the top of Sam's dresser. A bat bag stood in the corner, worn and dirty from heavy use. Trevor could just imagine the games and the tournaments, the crack of bats, the shouts of teammates, and the dusty tramp of feet over bases. He felt a shiver of joy before Sam's phone buzzed.

Trevor read the message and scowled, then his face relaxed. He typed furiously, explaining to McKenna what he needed. When the phone buzzed again, he smiled at McKenna's reply. She would get her publicist to help. Trevor wasn't crazy about the woman, but she did seem devoted to McKenna.

Trevor texted McKenna back that it was a good plan and asked her to send him a text, pretending he was Sam and saying that she wanted to help get his father's script green-lighted. She replied in less than a minute. Trevor forwarded McKenna's newest text to Sam, adding:

> lk what McK sent me 2 shw ur dad
> we'll get his script 2 b a movie!
> just gv me th wknd 2 play bball!

Trevor read McKenna's part over again, sent it to Sam, and walked down the hallway to show Sam's dad the phony text he got from McKenna.

Trevor filled his voice with excitement. "Dad, check it out. It's from McKenna Steele."

Sam's dad typed a few more lines, removed the pipe from his mouth, and spun around in the squeaky metal chair, taking the phone and reading the text. His eyebrows shot up. "McKenna Steele sent this? She's going to give my script to Trevor Goldman? He wants to help now? She's that close with him? Is this what you two talked about?"

"I wasn't sure. She said she wanted to think about it, but how good is this?" Trevor added an extra dash of excitement to his voice.

Sam's dad looked up and blinked. "I won't do it."

Trevor's insides froze.

22

SAM

Sam got up and wandered through the house, sneaking around and feeling like a thief. He slipped out the front door into the cool night. The air made him want to run, but what Trevor said about *Dark Cellar* made him fight the urge. He had to take advantage of the situation to help his dad. It was a once-in-a-lifetime opportunity.

He tiptoed down the walkway. A sudden hissing made his heart break into a gallop. Sprinklers. The hissing became a steady chug, and Sam scurried not to get wet. He crossed the cobblestone driveway and rounded the garage, a building twice as big as most people's homes. On the other side, the batting cage waited like a crouching giant draped in black netting.

On a metal post was a switch. He flipped it, and white light flooded the cage. The pitching machine hummed to life. Sam slipped through the netting and into the cage. He took a bat from the rack, stepped on the foot pedal, and blasted the first pitch that came at him. He hit righty for a while, then switched over, remembering that he never discussed the ability to switch-hit with Trevor and doubting that someone who never played in a league possessed such a skill. Sam made a mental note to warn Trevor to be ready with some excuse if the coach told him to bat lefty.

Sam kept the pitches coming and he kept swinging until the machine spit air. He removed the basket from the machine and began to fill it with the yellow rubber balls scattered across the concrete floor inside the cage. He reloaded the machine and stepped back into place, swinging and smashing the balls into the net in a steady rhythm that left him glazed with sweat and feeling almost comfortable. After the last pitch, he stood for a moment breathing.

Someone sniffed and Sam spun around.

Trevor's mom stood in bare feet wearing a dress red as a fire engine. In one hand was a champagne glass, in the other a pair of shiny black high-heeled shoes. Her hair looked out of place, and her eye makeup was smudged. Her eyes glistened with tears.

She scowled at Sam.

"Why are you doing this to me?"

Sam swallowed. "What am I doing?"

Trevor's mom narrowed her eyes. "You know exactly what you're doing."

23

TREVOR

Trevor finally found his voice. "Won't do what?"

Sam's dad's eyes glazed over. He guided the pipe stem toward his mouth and missed, hitting his chin and then his cheek before finding it with his teeth, clenching down, and nodding. "They can't toy with us. Blackballing us one minute, helping get a green light the next. No, I won't do it."

Trevor couldn't help the short burst of laughter. "You're kidding, right?"

Sam's dad scowled. He fished through his desk and held up a copy of *Dark Cellar*. "This is no joke. This is old-school horror. A classic in the making. Do you know how many people are interested in this? Do you know who I'm meeting tomorrow? Evan Tuttle, an associate in Jerry Bruckheimer's production company. Bruckheimer. What do you think of that?"

"Bruckheimer doesn't do horror . . . Dad."

"What about *Cat People*? Tuttle says Jerry is a big fan of horror. He loved doing *Cat People*. Trevor Goldman." Sam's dad spit the name out. "Who is he? Hollywood royalty. We don't need him. You think James Cameron needed a father to make him famous? Steven Spielberg? H. P. Lovecraft? Orson Welles? *They* were all originals, and so am I, Sam. So am I. Trevor Goldman has us blackballed one minute and we're going to go crawling to him the next? No siree."

Trevor winced at the burning words and retreated from the office. He wanted to shout at Sam's dad for being such a fool and tell him that was probably why he'd never gotten a script done and why he never would, either. But that wouldn't help Trevor play baseball. He grit his teeth and kept going.

"What's the matter?" Sam's dad asked.

Trevor got himself under control. He spoke without turning around. "Just trying to help, Dad."

Sam's dad followed him down the short hall. Trevor threw himself on the bed and scooped up the book. Sam's dad stood in the doorway and lit his pipe, blowing the smoke outside the room.

"I'm going to make it, Sam, and when I do, I'll make it because of me."

"Dad, that's how this town works. You take every opportunity you get. Who cares if Trevor Goldman had us blackballed? If he wants to help, we should let him. It's McKenna Steele who's really helping. I can't believe you're letting pride get in the way of *Dark Cellar*."

Sam's dad puffed on his pipe, shrugged, and sighed. "You'll understand one day, Sam."

Sam's dad closed the door and Trevor heard his footsteps moving back down the hall. He put the book down and turned out the light, but his mind stayed awake. He felt for the bat bag in the corner of the room and removed the mitt.

The glove felt like a natural part of his body. It fit perfectly and was as smooth as butter. He was determined to use it, and not just in tomorrow morning's practice. He had to figure a way to get that script into Sam's hands so that Sam could get working on the deal as Trevor Goldman. Once he got it going with Trevor's agent and manager, things would be so exciting that Sam wouldn't dream of switching back. Whatever happened after that—whether the movie got made or not—didn't really matter. If Sam's dad was too bullheaded to take the help, well, the world was full of fools.

All Trevor had to do was get that script and have it delivered to McKenna, and he'd be set to play in Saturday's game. If he was at home in Bel Air, he could give a job like that to Gabriel or Dolph or just dial up his agent, who'd come running. But as Sam Palomaki, he had no driver, no assistant, and certainly no agent.

He'd have to think of something else.

24

SAM

The only thing that kept Sam from running was the net. He stepped back.

"Stop pretending," Trevor's mom said. "I can't stand it."

Sam said nothing.

"You should be in bed." She spoke as if Sam had asked a question. "Baseball. Can you ever stop this? You have everything. Look."

She spun around, opening her arms in the direction of the huge mansion, before turning back to him. "Everything anyone could ever ask for. Everything that matters, but you want to play games. And you have to remind me of your obsession by banging around here after midnight when you've got work tomorrow."

She waited, and Sam knew she expected him to say something. He felt sure this was part of an ongoing argument and even considered a reply, but he just couldn't.

She raised her eyebrows. "No? Now you're playing the part of a mute? You can't talk? People think that's an easy role to play, but we know you have to say things with your expressions, no words, and in fact it's a difficult role. But look at you. What did Pierce Everette say? Beautiful. He's right. I almost believe you're scared and confused, but we both know, don't we? *Trevor*."

Sam just stood.

Her lips trembled. She huffed and threw her shoes into the bushes, then stamped off in her bare feet. Sam didn't move for several minutes. Finally, he left the cage, taking small, quiet steps on his way back to Trevor's bedroom. He paced the room until his eyes began to close, then lay down on the bed to fall asleep.

Heavy knocking woke him. Sunlight spilled into the room.

"Master Trevor?" From the accent, Sam knew it was the butler. "Master Trevor, Gabriel is downstairs. Your mother is in the breakfast room."

Sam jumped up and quickly used the bathroom. He pulled on a T-shirt, then grabbed the Nolan Ryan jersey, put it on as well, and flung open the door. The butler stood waiting patiently. He gave Sam a strange look, then walked away. Sam followed him, guessing that his next stop was the breakfast room. It was. Trevor's mom looked up from a cup of coffee with bleary eyes. She wore a turban and a white silk robe.

"I'm sorry," she said.

Sam offered her a small and hesitant smile, then shrugged. She smiled back.

"Good," she said. "Eat. Please."

Sam nodded and took a plate, carefully lifting the silver covers and serving himself a bit of everything. When he sat down, he saw Trevor's mom looking at his plate.

"Part of your new role?" she asked.

Sam mustered all his will. "No."

"He speaks."

Sam glanced at her and tried to smile. Her phone rang and she picked it up and began talking and texting until Gabriel appeared in the doorway pointing at his watch. Trevor's mom signaled Sam to go, and he followed the assistant out of the breakfast room after having taken only a few mouthfuls of food.

"Don't even think about that batting cage," Gabriel said.

Sam followed him into the car, letting Gabriel open the door and thanking him for it. Gabriel looked at him funny, but only climbed into the other side and told the driver, Dolph, to go. When a huge German shepherd beside the driver spun around and started barking violently, Sam nearly jumped out of his pants.

Dolph uttered the name Wolf, then a command, and the dog went silent, but continued to whine.

"I so sorry, Mr. Trevor," Dolph said. "I not know what Wolf do."

Sam couldn't believe Trevor had neglected to tell him that his driver rode around with a killer dog named Wolf, but he took some deep breaths and relaxed when it was apparent that the dog was under the driver's complete command.

When they stopped at a light, Dolph cleared his throat and looked at Sam in the rearview mirror.

The driver held up a glossy photo and spoke in a calm, quiet voice with an eastern European accent. "Mr. Trevor, please you sign this? My wife raise money fight cancer. Yes?"

"Dolph!" Gabriel barked. "You know we don't do that. How would you like it if I told Mrs. Goldman? What do you think she'd do?"

Sam sat, frozen, because he wanted to sign the picture, but he had no idea what Trevor's signature looked like.

"You see?" Gabriel scowled. "You made him feel uncomfortable. Trevor, I have to insist, just on principle."

Sam could only nod, but he felt like a rat. Dolph said nothing more, he just drove. Then Sam got an idea.

25

SAM

Sam pulled the Nolan Ryan jersey off over his head, folded it, and got out of his seat to hand it up over the back of the front seat, keeping a watchful eye on Wolf. He might not have done it if Trevor didn't have two of them, but since he did, Sam felt like it would be okay.

"Maybe my autograph is against the rules, Dolph," Sam said, "but there's nothing against me giving you one of my jerseys for your fundraiser, right?"

Gabriel gasped. "That jersey's got to be worth five thousand dollars; you can't just give that to Dolph."

"Why not?" It was Sam's turn to scowl. "It's charity. Aren't we supposed to be charitable? Who's against that?"

Dolph spoke very soft. "I like to return you favor one day. I like very much."

Dolph went silent, keeping his eyes straight ahead, but he did reach over to put the jersey on his lap in order to claim it. Wolf continued to whine in his throat. Gabriel sat back and sucked on his teeth. As if it were the only retort he was allowed to make, Gabriel snapped several sheets of paper from his briefcase and thrust them at him. Sam looked at the pages, then back at Gabriel, who was already at work on his BlackBerry, ignoring him. It didn't take Sam long to realize that the papers were scenes that he would be expected to perform once they got to the studio.

Sam's stomach turned. He took out his phone and texted Trevor, asking what he was supposed to do. No answer came back. Sam leafed through the pages, trying to concentrate. They arrived at the studio within minutes. Gabriel opened the big metal door and Sam let him hold it before heading toward where he knew Trevor's dressing room was.

"I'll be here if you need me and I'll send makeup in, in about twenty minutes." Gabriel sat down on one of two chairs in the hallway and continued on his BlackBerry.

Sam slipped inside the dressing room and closed the door behind him. He jumped when he realized he wasn't alone. McKenna sat waiting for him on the couch.

"Didn't mean to scare you, but I couldn't wait to see you." McKenna checked outside, said hello to Gabriel, shut the door again, and clapped her hands. She talked in a whisper. Her face glowed.

"How *was* it?"

"Scary. No one told me about Wolf. What the heck is that?"

McKenna waved a hand in the air. "Wolf's a sweetie. He's just for show."

"I swear, he knows I'm not Trevor."

96

"Doesn't matter," McKenna said. "The dog would jump off a cliff if Dolph told him to."

"His mom's scary, too." Sam told her everything that happened.

"She drinks at night," McKenna said. "Too much. Did you like the house? Isn't it incredible?"

"It's big," Sam said. "I can't believe he's got his own batting cage."

"Did you see the bowling alley or the soda fountain? The pool changes colors at night with all these lights under the water. And how about the waterfall?"

Sam shook his head. "Just his room and the main parts of the house."

"You know what we'll do?" McKenna's eyes went wide. "I'll go back with you today and show you everything. How about that?"

"That would be great."

"This is so fun." McKenna widened her eyes.

"Not really."

"Oh, relax." She held up a hand and flipped it down to scold him. "You've got to enjoy it."

Sam showed her his script. "I can't do this."

She laughed. "Sure you can. This is barely an acting job. Look at these lines. 'Hurry, or they'll kill us,' how tough is that? I swear they have some real dummies writing this stuff. Go ahead, try it."

"Hurry . . . or . . . they'll kill us."

"Yeah, well, okay." McKenna frowned. "I see what you mean. Put a little spark into it, right? Say it like you mean it.

You've got to pretend something."

"Pretend what?"

"Something. Like—I don't know—what'll happen if they find out you're not really Trevor. Pretend Trevor's mom finds out you're not him and she sics Wolf on you. Then say it. 'Hurry, or they'll kill us!'"

"Is the birthmark off?" Sam gripped his neck.

"No, but you look pretty upset. That'll work."

"She wouldn't do that with Wolf. They wouldn't *kill* us."

"Not actually."

"Even be too crazy mad, right?"

McKenna looked at the door and shrugged. "She'd be pretty mad, I'd think, but I doubt they'd charge your dad with kidnapping."

"Kidnapping? What are you talking about?"

26

TREVOR

Trevor woke and had to think a minute to remember where he was. Instead of jasmine filling the air with its sweet-smelling flowers, the smell of garbage crept into his nose, wrinkling it. The only birds outside didn't twitter or sing. They were black crows, and they croaked and cawed and seemed to be laughing. At him?

He picked up one of Sam's trophies and felt its cool, smooth touch to convince himself that it was all really happening and remind himself that today he'd be living out a dream. He changed into a pair of red athletic shorts and a black T-shirt that had real holes in it. He tugged it on, happy with its softness and knowing that the holes were the perfect costume detail for the movie role of a poor kid about to launch himself into a pro baseball career. That reminded him to freshen up the makeup on his exposed skin to lighten its color a bit and play his part.

Finished, he slipped Sam's mitt onto his hand. The thrill that buzzed through him was no acting job. He really felt it, and the sensation stayed with him as he charged into the tiny kitchen, sitting down next to Sam's dad and staring at the cereal box in front of him.

He watched Sam's dad for only half a minute before realizing the box of cereal, carton of milk, and bottle of orange juice was it: breakfast. The bowl in front of him was made of wax-covered paper and the spoon, like the tabletop, was plastic. Trevor remembered a movie scene he'd done about a poor boy in the rural South who owned a dog who got him into all kinds of trouble. In one scene, the boy poured his own cereal and milk and started reading the sports scores at the table, so that's what Trevor did, to perfection.

When Trevor finished and looked up from his cereal bowl and the newspaper, Sam's dad was staring at him. "It's really incredible. I swear, I Googled Trevor Goldman on my computer this morning, and Sam, you're like his identical twin. I never really thought about it too much, I mean until you cut your hair, it wasn't as completely obvious as it is now, but if your skin was darker, I'm telling you. . . ."

Sam's dad continued to stare until Trevor shifted in his seat. "Well, I got practice, so . . ."

"Sam." Sam's dad reached over and put a hand on Trevor's arm. "I know we don't talk about it, but you know you were adopted. I can't help wondering if this Trevor Goldman might not *be* your twin."

Trevor swallowed. "Do I have a twin? Is that something you knew about?"

Sam's dad shook his head and Trevor felt relieved. He would hate to think his own parents actually knew about a twin and never told him.

"But I think Diana Goldman might know."

Trevor felt ill. "Why would you say that?"

Sam's father wrinkled up half his face. "I think that's what happened at the studio. I think someone who knew saw you and realized. I can't imagine what they'd do if they saw you now. That would be something."

Sam's father broke into a grin.

"But we don't want to make any trouble, right?" Trevor chose his words carefully. "Because they could really make it hard for you to get your script green-lighted."

Sam's dad pinched his own chin between thumb and pointer finger. "They could. No, we'll leave well enough alone, but it's another good reason for you not to let McKenna Steele try to get Trevor Goldman to help you with *Dark Cellar*. It could blow up in our faces, and I seriously doubt two kids could get it the right attention."

Trevor kept quiet during the ride to practice. When they pulled into the parking lot of the school where Sam's team was already taking the field, his heart began to dance. Players dotted the grass with blue caps matching the one he had taken from Sam's dresser top. The car stopped. Trevor tugged on the cap and swung open the door.

"Hey!"

Trevor spun, wondering what could have upset Sam's dad so much.

"No hug?"

101

Trevor looked at him with doubt. He felt certain he must have hugged his own father, but he just couldn't say for sure and he certainly didn't *remember* doing it, if in fact he really did. Even his mother was pretty thin when it came to hugs unless someone was taking pictures.

"Don't tell me you think you're going to get away without a hug," Sam's father said, getting out of the car. "Come here."

Trevor knew about hugs from his work as an actor, and he gave Sam's dad one even though it felt very different than something from a movie scene. When Sam's dad kissed Trevor's cheek, he felt his face go warm. He turned away quickly.

"Okay, Dad, see you in a while."

"Okay, Sam. I've got one of those English as a second language classes down at the center. I got fifty new kids today I'm going to try to get started on reading, but when I come back to get you, I'll have a surprise."

Trevor nodded but kept going, hungry to practice and eager to get the first interaction with Sam's teammates over with so he knew what he'd be dealing with.

"Sam, thanks for coming!" Coach Sharp shouted. "Whoa! That's some haircut, Palomaki. Glad to finally see your face. Two ears? Didn't know you even had ears."

The coach grinned at him, then went back to his discussion with the three assistant coaches.

Trevor knew who was who just from Sam's descriptions. Besides the coach, he recognized Cole Price by his dark hair and wire frame glasses, Frankie and RJ Schmelling—Frankie by the red hair, his brother because he was bigger than anyone except Dorian Klum. Trevor knew RJ wasn't Klum because

Klum had blond hair like Trevor and RJ's hair was black.

Trevor jogged up to a group of players gathered around the bench.

"Hey, Sam," Frankie said.

"Hey, Frankie."

"Hey, Sam," said a boy Trevor couldn't recognize from any of Sam's descriptions.

"Hey, what's going on." Trevor covered his tracks with the universal reply.

A hand gripped the back of Trevor's arm from behind, pinching his skin in a horse bite. "What's going on is you thinking you can show up late 'cause you're coach's little pet, Palomaki."

Trevor whipped his arm free and spun around.

Staring hard at him was Dorian Klum, and he was even bigger than Sam had described him. Snickering and standing right next to Klum was the pudgy boy Sam had described as Klum's only friend, Scotty Needum. Trevor's mind whirled. He knew he had to do something. He couldn't let Klum treat him that way without a response.

He'd acted out a fight in a movie called *David Copperfield*, but in the movie, he knew they weren't really going to hit each other, only pretend. The look in Klum's eyes told Trevor that now he had to prepare for the real thing.

Trevor balled up his fists and butterflies swirled in his stomach.

27

SAM

Sam stared at McKenna, urging her with his expression to explain.

"I'm just thinking worst case," she said.

"That's insane."

"I'm sure it won't happen."

"It can't happen." Sam shook his head. "That's not true."

"It might look bad, is all. People get hysterical sometimes, but you're getting the idea. You've got the spark now. Try saying the lines."

Sam stared at her, then he huffed and said them.

"Not bad." She laughed. "You're a natural."

Sam shook his head. "I told Trevor I wanted to call it quits last night, but he said all I have to do is make it to the weekend. He plays one game of baseball, and meantime I get my dad's script into the hands of his agent. You're going to help

104

me with that, right? Tell me what to do?"

"That? That's easy."

"How?"

"How? Just call Stu Lisson. He's your agent. Tell him to get over here 'cause you've got a script you want him to see. Tell him you're behind it. You want to see it made."

"That's it?" Sam had been waiting for some kind of magic words. "'I'm behind it'?"

"You're Trevor Goldman."

"Right. I am. To him, right?"

"That's all it takes."

"But we have to get the script." Sam bit his lower lip.

"I'm taking care of that." McKenna pointed at herself with a thumb. "We worked out the details last night."

"What details?"

"I made some calls and found out the producer your dad met with, a guy named Paul Gertz." McKenna shrugged. "I called Sara Grant, and she's going to grab it for us."

"Who's Sara Grant?"

"My publicist."

"Oh."

"I know it sounds crazy, but I trust her."

"Why is it crazy?"

"She's a publicist. People don't trust publicists, but Sara is great. She got me that *Teen Beat* cover shot and feature story."

Sam wasn't sure, but he guessed that was one of the magazines girls his age sometimes read. He'd seen them in the grocery store. He'd seen McKenna's face on plenty of them but didn't know the magazines' exact names.

"Why don't they trust publicists?"

"Well, think about it," McKenna said. "If Sara figured this all out and she leaked it? Think how much publicity that would generate. It'd be huge. A scandal. You'd be famous, and I'd be even more famous. Me being famous is her job, so . . ."

McKenna's phone buzzed and she checked the message.

"But you don't think she'd do that?"

"Well, she's here. She just texted me. I don't think so, but the best thing would be for her not to know, so try not to blow it."

"Blow it?"

"Your cover. Act like Trevor."

"How?"

There was a knock at the dressing room door.

"I don't know." McKenna threw up her hands, reaching for the doorknob. "Just be nice, but not too nice. Trevor doesn't really like Sara."

Sam opened his mouth to ask more questions, but before he could say another word, McKenna flung open the door and there stood the heavy woman with the black glasses, sharp nose, and bright red hair who had farted so loudly in the Central Casting stairwell.

Sam remembered the embarrassing and hilarious moment and couldn't contain a burst of laughter. But at the sound of his laugh, the woman's face changed. She looked directly into his eyes and scowled so hard that her mouth curled into a sneer.

Sam remembered her words from the stairwell—"You'll get yours"—and he stopped laughing.

28

TREVOR

Klum shoved Trevor. He stumbled back, slipped, and thumped the ground on his backside. The other kids crowded around, hungry for the fight. Klum jutted out his chin, just daring Trevor to hit him.

Trevor sprang up and swung his fist.

Before impact, Trevor's eyes closed.

He felt an iron grip on his wrist, arresting the punch.

"Are you two crazy?" Coach Sharp screamed so loud it hurt Trevor's ears.

Trevor stumbled sideways, off balance, but the coach held him up and kept him from falling again.

"He started it." Trevor blurted out the words, pointing at Klum, whose look had gone from angry attacker to one of an almost innocent bystander.

"Nah," Scotty Needum said. "Palomaki started it."

"I told him he can't show up late and think it's okay, Coach," Klum said. "You asked us to show leadership, and being late is garbage. You say that."

"You don't just shove someone," Trevor said. "That's not being a leader, that's being a thug."

"You tried to throw a punch. Tried." Klum's smile mocked Trevor's swing.

Scotty Needum laughed and a couple of other kids joined in, despite the general feeling Trevor could sense against Klum.

"I don't want any of this," Coach Sharp said. "You guys have that much energy? Get on the baseline. We've got a long practice, but if you're that full of vinegar, you can all run."

The team groaned but lined up as the coach said, sprinting from the first base line, across the infield to the third base line, and back to the tune of their coach's whistle. Both Trevor and Klum drew angry stares between whistles, and by the time it was over, no one was able to stand upright or catch his breath. Trevor wiped the sweat from his face, ready to vomit.

"You woulda smashed him like a bug," Cole said between gasps. "He's lucky Coach stopped it, but I can't believe you actually took a swing at him."

"What was I supposed to do?" Trevor asked.

Joey gave him a funny look. "Well you never messed with him before. He's always pushing us around."

Trevor grasped for the right words. "And why does he do it? Because we let him."

"Because we all know he's crazy," Cole said. "Or did you forget Brian Leonard?"

"No," Trevor said, his mind grasping for details Sam might

have told him about a boy named Brian Leonard.

"Because no one wants *that* to happen to them."

Trevor realized that Cole was staring at him, expecting a response.

"No," Trevor said, wondering what horror Klum had committed on the boy named Brian Leonard. "No, you're right. No one wants that."

"So," Cole asked, "what are you planning to do to keep him from doing it to you?"

29

SAM

Sam felt like McKenna's publicist knew his secret for sure. Her look didn't waver; it came at him like an X-ray.

"Oh, I know why you think you can laugh." Sara kept glaring.

Sam swallowed. He figured the safest thing to say was nothing.

"You think this is all a big joke." Sara frowned, but she held up the script Sam's dad had written. "You don't care about some monster movie. You just want to see me hustle around for you, like some practical joke."

"That's not true, Sara. I really want it." McKenna snatched the script from her and handed it to Trevor. "It's my idea. We watched a scary movie the other day at my house and started talking about it. . . . "

"But *that*? *Dark Cellar* by Randall Palomaki?" Even though

Sara's voice had turned moderately pleasant, she never let her eyes waver from Sam. "Who is Randall Palomaki? I never even heard of the guy."

"I was talking with one of the PAs about scary movies, and she said she heard about this wicked hot script," McKenna said.

"Hot?" Sara said. "The only heat on that script is gonna come from an incinerator."

"Can you keep a secret?" McKenna asked.

Sara's eyes widened for a moment. "Don't be ridiculous. What publicist can't keep a secret? I'd be out of a job."

McKenna leaned toward her and lowered her voice. "We've got Trevor's dad involved."

Sara studied Sam. "His dad?"

"Yes."

"Any secret involving Trevor's dad is a secret worth keeping, don't you think?" The publicist's eyes never left Sam.

"You're the best." McKenna turned her toward the door and patted the heavyset publicist on the back.

"We all know that, darling," Sara said, and she stroked McKenna's head before she turned to go. "Good-bye. Trevor."

"See you," Sam said, waving even though Sara was already out through the dressing room door.

McKenna closed it behind her and held up the script. "We got it."

"She knows." Sam buried his head in his hands.

"Knows what?"

"She *knows*. Did you see how she looked at me? And that stuff about keeping a secret. I couldn't even speak. I had no idea what to say. This isn't working."

"No, you were great. Polite, but not gushing over her. I think Trevor would have scowled back at her a little more; maybe you could do that, but it's all good."

"Scowl? I almost wet my pants."

"Stop fooling around. Now we call your agent and get a deal going for your father's script."

30

TREVOR

Since Trevor didn't know what Klum had done to the boy named Brian Leonard, he had no reply for Cole's question. Coach Sharp's whistle tweeted, saving him from having to answer. Instead, he hustled into action with the rest of the team, smiling all the while. First they loosened their arms, working their way to a long ball throw before doing a series of defensive drills that included scooping up grounders and firing the ball to first, snagging pop flies, and working situations around the infield. Trevor's favorite was the double play drill. Since Sam's position was shortstop, Trevor got to both throw to second and cover the bag if the ball got fielded by the second baseman. The body positioning, steps, and techniques of catching the ball not just to catch it, but to make the fastest throw possible, got Trevor's blood racing.

When Trevor was actually able to scoop a grounder, tag

second himself, and then make the throw to first, he almost burst with pride, until Frankie—who'd caught his throw to first—began to chuckle.

"What?" Trevor couldn't help from asking.

"You're goofing on me."

Trevor hid his confusion with a smile and a nod, but the next time he threw to first, Frankie didn't laugh.

"Come on, Sam," Frankie said. "Stop with the wild throws. Put it in my mitt. Practice like you play."

"Where do you want it?" Trevor blurted out the question.

"Right here." Frankie held out his glove, chest high. "Not here or here." Frankie moved his glove down near his ankles, then up over his head, the two places Trevor's throws had gone.

Trevor nodded like he knew all along, but, try as he might, he couldn't make the throw with the kind of accuracy Frankie was used to from Sam. Since Frankie said nothing more about it, though, Trevor relaxed and again began to enjoy the practice.

When they changed over to a pop fly drill and Coach Sharp called Trevor over for a private word, he couldn't help beaming at the coach. It was the first time he'd ever interacted with other players in this way and it felt so natural and good—it was everything he'd always imagined.

"Uh, Sam," the coach said, putting an arm around Trevor's shoulder, "you okay?"

Trevor blinked up at the coach. "Sure. What do you mean?"

The coach shrugged. "Okay. Everyone has an off day, right?"

Trevor felt his insides twist. He couldn't help from speaking. "What do you mean?"

The coach chuckled and mussed Trevor's hat. "Go on, stop

biffing me. You and I both know that wasn't the real Sam Palomaki I just saw."

Trevor remembered Frankie's complaint, and his insides went cold. If he was discovered, he'd never get to play in tomorrow's game. He had to play in that game. He quickly and coldly calculated what had happened: As good as he thought he was, he was no Sam Palomaki. So, the right thing to do was go along with what Coach Sharp wanted to believe, that Sam was having an off day.

Trevor grinned and tried to sound as casual as he could. "It's not the Sam Palomaki you'll see in the game tomorrow, Coach. That's for sure."

The coach grinned back. "Good. Get back out there."

Trevor ran and caught and threw for all he was worth while at the same time acting like he couldn't believe how poor his practice was. When the outfielders who'd been working their bats switched over to the field, Trevor and his group began to work on their offense. Trevor went through a series of drills, swinging bats and sometimes even broomsticks at not only baseballs but a ball on a rope and Ping-Pong-ball-sized Wiffle balls. Again, Trevor felt proud of how well he connected with almost everything he swung at, but he was more careful this time not to act too joyful.

Practice ended with everyone taking turns hitting against a live defense. Each batter got three at bats with ten pitches each. If you hit it, you ran and took as much as you could get from the defense. Coach Sharp had a scoring system based on hits, strikes, and balls. The winner would get a bag of M&M's, not a huge prize but something fun that Trevor was eager to win.

Trevor got to go first. He removed the bat from Sam's bag and approached the plate. He was almost there before he realized he'd be batting against Klum. With everything that had been running through his mind and his struggle to perform, Trevor had forgotten about Klum and his promise of revenge. He had also been too busy to worm the information out of anyone about Brian Leonard and discover what horror Klum had committed. But Trevor pushed all that from his mind. He was more worried about hitting the ball as well as Sam, who was the team's best batter, to keep Coach Sharp from suspecting anything more than he already did.

Trevor swung a few times, getting his groove, then stepped into the batter's box, crouching and cocking his bat back. He forced himself to look confident, even bold, despite the tremor in his upper lip.

Klum smirked from the mound, wound up, and threw a screaming fastball . . . right at Trevor's face.

31
SAM

Sam scratched his ear. "What's the agent's name again?"

"Stu Lisson." McKenna took Trevor's phone from Sam and punched up Stu's number on the speed dial without hitting Send. "Same as mine. That's how we met, remember? I heard Trevor tell you that."

"You mean that's how you and Trevor met."

"Right, but now you're him, so *we* met through our agent at a cast party for Miley Cyrus. Here."

Sam took the phone. "And what do I say? I mean, how does Trevor talk to this guy?"

"They're buddies. Stu knows everyone inside the business. Trevor's dad picked him, but Trevor loves him, so just be nice."

"So, like, 'Hey, Mr. Lisson—'"

117

"Hey, *Stu*; Trevor calls him Stu. I call him Stu. Everyone calls him Stu."

"So, 'Hey, Stu, I've got this script you've got to see. I'm behind it, and I want to see if you can get someone to make it'? Is that all I say?"

McKenna seemed to be weighing his words. "I think you say it a little more forcefully, and you tell Stu he's going to *love* it and you *know* it's going to be a blockbuster. Tell him you're behind it. Let me ask you, is there a girl my age in *Dark Cellar*?"

"Yes, the daughter. It's a great part. She's the only one who lives."

"Perfect. Tell him you know McKenna loves it and that she's dying to play the daughter. Say it like you've got a thing for me."

"A thing?"

"You know, like if Trevor liked me, if he cared, and wanted to make me happy."

Sam didn't think before he spoke. "Does he?"

McKenna shook her head. "Not really. Not like that. I mean, we're friends."

"But you wanted him to have a 'thing' for you?"

"I don't know. Maybe. Not anymore." McKenna let her words hang in the air like big soap bubbles.

Sam felt his face heat up. He looked away, afraid to ask if the reason was him, even though he dared to dream it was. He hoped it so much that his chest ached, and that made it too scary to talk about.

A knock on the dressing room door saved him.

"Come in," McKenna said.

The makeup artist peeked her head in and asked if Sam was ready.

"Sure," he said.

The makeup artist went to the counter in front of the brightly lit mirror and began unpacking a box that looked to Sam like it should hold fishing lures. When she had everything out and ready, she turned and looked from Sam to the barber chair in front of her. "Okay?"

Sam looked at McKenna, who angled her head toward the chair.

"Sure." Sam sat down.

The makeup artist looked at Sam's face in the mirror and began to apply some makeup with a soft round pad.

"Um, Trevor," she said as she dabbed at the back of his neck, "I think there's something . . . I guess something wrong . . . with your birthmark."

32

SAM

"I don't think you should be asking Trevor about his birth-mark," McKenna said, blurting out the words and scowling at the makeup artist.

The artist's face turned red. "I'm sorry. It's just that it looks like it might be changing. Maybe he should have a doctor look at it."

McKenna hesitated a beat, then said, "He is having a doc-tor look at it. That's why it's not polite. He doesn't want to talk about it, right, Trevor?"

Sam wasn't used to being bold with people, but he under-stood that McKenna was trying to distract the woman so she might not realize that the birthmark wasn't the only thing that was different. He touched the back of his neck and did his best to sound offended. "No, I really don't want to talk about it."

The artist's back went rigid and she chewed on her lower

lip, seeming to consider whether or not to get into a verbal battle with McKenna. Finally, she huffed and shook her head and continued with the makeup, brushing it on with quick little strokes. "Fine."

Sam let the woman finish her job. Just as she finished, a knock at the door was followed by several people from wardrobe, who helped him into a suit of samurai battle armor. There was so much activity, Sam almost forgot to be nervous. With every passing minute, it seemed the number of people orbiting him grew. Finally, they had him ready and he walked in the midst of the small crowd toward the set.

Through it all, McKenna stayed by his side, smiling and nodding with encouragement. Before he knew it, Sam stood on a rock cliff with a huge green screen as the backdrop. A young Asian woman was already on her spot. Pierce Everette, the director, quickly appeared and put an arm around both Sam and the beautiful woman who Sam knew was his mother in the movie.

"Okay, Trevor, this is the scene where Kiku tells you who your father is. As you listen, the mystery of your entire life is finally answered. Then you hear horse hoofs. You both look. You're shocked. You hit your line. The two of you clasp hands, and you jump."

Sam looked over the edge of the cliff at the foam mat waiting not more than two feet below. He worked up his courage and put as much emotion into his voice as he could muster. "Hurry, or they'll kill us."

The director gave Sam a strange look, then smiled. "That's funny, Trevor. Obviously, you'll put some emotion into it."

121

Sam felt his jaw go slack. He put a hand to his mouth and fought to keep his stomach from turning inside out.

"Okay, we all set?" the director asked.

Kiku nodded and Sam, unable to think of anything else, did the same. The flurry of activity made his head spin, but all Sam could do was stare at the actor named Kiku. Her oval face seemed to float in the frame of her long black hair, and she stared intently at Sam.

Someone said something about the scene number and the take, held up a digital clapper board, and clacked it shut.

The director shouted, "Action!"

33

TREVOR

Trevor clenched his eyes shut and spun.

The ball thumped the meat of his back high up along his spine, knocking the wind out of him, sending him on a tumble into the catcher and raising a cloud of dust. Trevor's hands and feet tingled.

Coach Sharp hovered over him. "Sam. Sam? You okay?"

Trevor wiped his eyes and sniffed and tried to stand. Pain stabbed his back, but he grit his teeth and got up with the coach's help, flexing his hands and feet.

"You okay?" The coach looked into his eyes.

Trevor nodded and bit his lip. He didn't want to cry, but the pain and the shame and the shock of someone actually trying to hurt him sent a charge through his body that he wasn't used to.

Coach Sharp's face wrinkled with rage. "Klum! You know

better! Get out! Go! You're done!"

The coach stabbed his finger toward the parking lot.

"Coach, it was a wild pitch. I lost control." Klum was a terrible actor, and Trevor was glad to see that the coach wasn't buying it.

"Go home and think about it. Go, before I kick you off this team for good."

Klum scowled and threw his glove and stomped off.

The catcher dusted himself off and spoke under his breath. "Jerk."

Trevor looked and felt a wave of relief when he realized the catcher was talking about Klum and not him.

"Maybe that'll teach him," the coach said. "Curtis, take the mound!"

A new pitcher jogged out onto the infield and snatched the ball Coach Sharp tossed him.

"You okay to hit?" the coach asked.

Trevor nodded and adjusted his batting helmet, still shaken from the pitch that had almost smashed his face and left what he knew would be a brutal welt on his back. He stepped into the batter's box. Curtis nodded, wound up, and threw.

Trevor watched the ball, low and fast but straight as a pitching machine. He started to grin even before he connected with the ball. The bat cracked, and everyone's head turned to watch the hit fly for the left field fence. Trevor took off, fueled by an excitement he'd never known.

The ball didn't clear the fence, and as Trevor rounded first, he saw the left fielder snatch it up and rifle the ball toward second base. Trevor leaned into his stride, then slid ten feet from the bag. The ball smacked into the second baseman's mitt, shocking Trevor with its accuracy, but his slide was picture-perfect and he passed under the tag.

In that instant, Trevor recounted the hundreds—maybe even thousands—of times he'd slid into a base on a patch of yard down behind the house where he worked with his baseball coach. He could see his mom's scowling face when she asked what in the world he was doing, and the sour look she gave his coach when he told her one of the fundamentals every baseball player had to learn was the skill of sliding. That was the first time he heard his mom say that he wasn't a baseball player, he was a thespian, which was just some fancy name for an actor.

"Safe!" Coach Sharp bellowed from behind the plate. "Great hit. Great slide! Now you're back on your game, Sam!"

Trevor popped up on top of the bag and smacked at his pants. An easy breeze carrying the smell of fresh-cut grass on its back swept the dust away. The sun shone down, warming him through and through. It was the perfect moment, and it took all of his acting skills not to laugh out loud with joy.

34
SAM

Sam's mouth continued to hang open as Kiku dove into the story of his character's past: the father, captain of a great ship from across the sea gone off to fight on the vast ocean, protecting them from brutal invaders, and his grandfather's disapproval, then gradual acceptance of Sam's character as heir to the empire. Sam actually listened to it as though it were true, and so, when she finished, he stared blankly for several beats before the director shouted, "Trevor, let's go! Now you hear the horse's hoofs! They're coming for you! Give it to me!"

Startled, the whole thing came crashing down on Sam—him faking to be Trevor, Trevor faking to be him, the scam to try and get a deal for his dad's script, and the near certainty they'd be caught and his dad would somehow get arrested for kidnapping—it frightened him so badly that he meant it when he blurted out his lines.

126

"Hurry, or they'll kill us!"

Kiku clutched his hand and half dragged Sam to the edge of the cliff. She crouched and jumped, dragging him behind her. Sam couldn't do anything other than leap with her. They both sank safely into the foam two feet below.

"And . . . cut!" The director suddenly appeared, helping them both down off the foam landing pad. "My God, I loved it! Beautiful! Trevor, just beautiful! Your *shock*, your *disbelief*, it was *real*!"

Kiku patted Sam on the back. McKenna appeared with both thumbs up.

Sam laughed out loud.

35

TREVOR

The thrill for Trevor didn't last.

Although he knocked one of his first ten pitches against Curtis out of the park and hit a single as well, the next time Trevor got up to bat, a third pitcher had taken the mound, Tommy Graham. Trevor grinned and lazily swung his bat to warm up before stepping into the box. Graham wound up and in came the pitch. Trevor swung for the fences and was shocked to miss it by a mile.

Coach Sharp chuckled. "Stop fooling around, Sam."

Trevor's palms went damp, and he adjusted his grip on the bat. He could have sworn he would hit the pitch he just missed. Graham wound up and threw. Trevor swung. Nothing. Coach Sharp huffed. Trevor didn't even look back. He stepped out of the box and took a couple more practice swings. He went back at it, losing confidence with each try because every swing was a foul tip or a complete whiff.

Trevor only had one pitch left in his ten. This time, he glared at Graham, grit his teeth, and focused with all his might on the pitcher's hand, ready for the ball that would come at him.

Graham wound up and threw.

Trevor swung and missed, but he finally saw what was happening. He knew what the problem was. More than half the pitches Graham was throwing were curveballs. For all the countless hours Trevor spent hitting balls, he—or his coach—never bothered to adjust his machine to throw him curveballs. It was something they could easily have done but hadn't. Why would they? In the back of his mind, and probably his coach's, they'd both suspected that he would never really be allowed to play baseball.

His birthday present came to mind, and the bitter disappointment he'd felt during his fake "scrimmage" with the Dodgers.

"Honestly, Sam?" the coach said, shaking his head. "I sent Klum home for that pitch he threw at you, but at least Klum cares. He might be a bit wild, but he takes his baseball seriously. I really don't know what's up with you today. Maybe it's the haircut."

Even though Coach Sharp made light of the sudden drop-off in practice, Trevor knew he had to do something if he was going to keep his pinch hitting for Sam a secret. If the inconsistencies continued, the coach would talk to Sam's dad, and Sam's dad might put all the strange pieces together, completing the puzzle and making a clear picture of what they were up to.

The problem was that Trevor had no idea who to turn to.

McKenna wouldn't have any idea about curveballs. His coach would wonder why the sudden interest, and he'd want to *show* Trevor, not text him instructions. The perfect person was Sam, but that was a problem, too. Trevor wanted to have as little contact with Sam as he could for fear that Sam would pull the plug on the whole deal.

But as he walked to the dugout to return his bat to the rack, Trevor knew it had to be Sam. He fitted the bat into an open slot, then slipped Sam's phone out of the bat bag. Quickly, he sent his newfound twin a text:

how do u hit a curveball???

36
SAM

"You're a real piece of work." The director gripped Sam's shoulder. "Messing around with me like that, playing dumb, and then nailing your line. You're a real pro, my friend, a real pro."

The only thing Sam could think about was how easy it had been, easy and, now that he'd successfully gotten through it, *fun*. He couldn't imagine anything easier or more exciting than the clack of that clapper board, the emotional recitation of another actor's lines, and then hitting your own.

"I love this," Sam said without thinking.

"Of course you do," the director said. "It's in your blood."

Sam wondered about that. Of course, he said nothing, but when everyone left him alone in his dressing room (McKenna had lines in the next scene), he couldn't get the idea out of his mind. It was in his blood. Trevor was a natural actor, not because his father was a captain of Hollywood and his mother a movie star, but because whoever came before him (and Sam) had *acting* in their blood. Acting, and maybe baseball, too?

Sam stared at himself in the mirror, not at the features of his face, but into his own eyes. Shards of blue circled by a black rim with a deep pit in the center of the blue spokes. The pit expanded like a living thing, breathing in and out on its own. Sam felt drawn into those deep pits as if they were windows into the past that could teach him the secrets about his own life and the lives of others.

Sam had never wanted to know who his biological parents were. He'd never wondered about them. If he thought about them at all, it was like they were nameless, faceless, cutout cardboard figures. He knew who his parents were. His father was one of the best human beings on the planet, a man Sam loved with every fiber. His mom was a shadow he never knew, but even she had form and substance in Sam's mind, a ghost whose voice he could almost hear, pictures on the walls or in photo albums of Sam as a baby. Pictures that sometimes came to life.

But this, this idea was something new. It was a link between not only him and Trevor as twins, but then the two of them tethered back to two living, breathing human beings like matching balloons on a string. Eyes, hair, noses, moods, and yes, even talents that came directly from two people who were not only *real*, but *out there*. Somewhere, two people who created Sam and Trevor were walking around at that very moment. What were they doing? Who were they, and where?

Most of all, what would it be like to have a mother, a loving woman who cared about you no matter what you did or who you were, someone to hug you when you were beyond sad, or beyond happy? Sam had always felt an ache in his heart over his missing mother. It was another thing that he and his father shared. The ache he had now was something new—similar, but also different. He ached for the mother he had lost, but more than that, he now ached for the mother he'd never found.

That brought him to an idea that was as confusing as it was frightening: what if Sam—especially Sam in the role of Trevor Goldman, with uncounted money and power and fame—could actually reach out into the world . . . and *find* her?

Sam scooped up Trevor's phone off the dressing table to text Trevor and tell him what he planned to do. Before he did anything, though, he saw that a text from Trevor was already waiting for him.

37

TREVOR

Trevor took his turn in the field without the phone. One of the rules Sam had been very clear about was texting during practice.

"Coach Sharp will eat your liver if he catches you texting out on the field," Sam had said. "I'm serious. I've never seen him kick anyone off the team for good—even though he'll toss people out of practice for goofing around—but if he caught you texting, that'd be it. I'm sure."

Trevor tried to stay focused on playing defense but was probably lucky that nothing came his way. Finally, it was his third turn at bat. He jogged to the dugout, checked to see that the coach wasn't looking, and snuck a peek at Sam's phone. His spirits lifted when he saw he had a message from Sam, and he quickly opened the text.

curvbll is ez key is 2 c it. just look
4 red dot n keep ur wght n bat bk
till it breaks. fyi im going 2 find our
bio mom n dad

"Sam!"

Trevor heard the coach's shout but was so puzzled and horrified by the text that he forgot he was supposed to be Sam.

"Sam! Don't even tell me you're texting during practice!"

Trevor slipped the phone back into the bag and bolted up
out of the dugout with his bat. "No, Coach, just looking for a
stick of gum."

"Well, get up here, will you? I swear. . . ."

Trevor walked toward the plate, his brain overheating from
the part of the message about a biological mom and dad. Finding his biological parents was something Trevor never even
considered before, let alone actually setting out to find them.
Questions bombarded his brain. Could Sam actually find
them? How? Where were they? *Who* were they? His mind went
foggy, like it all had to be a dream, and Trevor realized that
Coach Sharp was losing patience with him. He pushed the
entire crazy idea from his mind.

Now it was time to be baffled by Sam's message about a red
dot. The part about keeping his weight and bat back until the
break, Trevor got that. It made sense. He wanted to swing at
the ball when it crossed the plate and swing accurately. If the
ball was going to drop and veer a bit to the outside of the plate,
he needed to stay back, watch it, and swing fast. Trevor knew

135

from his coach that he had a quick bat—at least, the coach always said so. So, he should be *able* to stay back.

It was the red dot that he didn't understand. Trevor had heard about batters who could read the spin of the ball and therefore recognize the type of pitch, but he'd never really worked on it since all his batting was done with the yellow rubber balls of the pitching machine. Trevor could hit them well and with a fast swing, but making the adjustment obviously wasn't going to be easy, and the first thing he had to do was *see* the pitch.

He took a couple practice swings, then a deep breath before he stepped into the box. Graham couldn't help but smile. He wound up and let the ball fly. In the white blur of the ball, Trevor saw it. He actually saw it! The faint illusion of a red dot created by the fast downward spin of the curveball. Trevor stayed back, waiting, swung, and missed.

The ball clapped into the catcher's mitt. Trevor looked back at Coach Sharp, who stood behind the plate with his arms crossed and a stern look on his face. Trevor grinned at him. "I saw it!"

The coach's face went slack. "Saw what?"

Trevor instantly realized that Sam, who could obviously hit a curveball with ease, wouldn't be excited about seeing the red dot. He wouldn't think twice about it.

"Just the pitch, Coach. My eyes have been bugging me. When I got my hair buzzed, the girl who did it bumped my eye," Trevor said, pointing to his left eye, "and it's a bit blurry, but I saw it this time. I'll be okay."

"She hit your eye?" The coach moved toward Trevor, looking with real concern. "Let me see."

The coach tilted Trevor's head back and examined his eye. "It looks okay."

"It's feeling better. I'm okay."

The coach got back behind the plate. This time, Trevor grinned right back at Graham. The ball came. Trevor saw the dot. He stayed back with his weight and his bat, waiting for the pitch to fall and drift.

When it did, he swung.

38

SAM

Sam put the phone down, worried that things might not be going so well for Trevor. If he was asking how to hit a curveball, Sam could only imagine the struggles he was having during practice.

"I bet Klum is loving it." Sam spoke aloud in the empty dressing room.

A knock on the door disturbed him.

"Come in."

Gabriel peeked around the edge of the door before walking in and handing Sam a sheet of paper with a schedule on it. "Your next scene isn't until after lunch. You've got a half hour of radio interviews from twelve-thirty until one."

"Interviews about what?" Sam asked.

Gabriel paused a beat, then said, "For *Bright Lights,* remember?"

Sam couldn't help looking confused at the list of radio stations and times in three- and five-minute segments.

"The studio publicist set up five half-hour blocks for release week. It's in your contract. Your father said it was okay, so . . ."

"Man," Sam said, realizing there were way too many things he didn't know, but figuring *Bright Lights* must be a movie Trevor was in that was coming out this week. "We shot that a while ago. I barely remember it."

"No, but you could probably tell me Matt Kemp's batting average, couldn't you?" Gabriel folded his arms across his chest before he pulled another sheet out of his shoulder bag. "Don't worry, I've got the press release right here and bullet points the studio asked you to stick to as much as you can."

Sam took the sheet and read the summary of the movie, a story about a young boy kidnapped by his own father, who escapes, gets lost, and ultimately is found after a series of adventures in New York City. The studio wanted him to use buzzwords like "heart wrenching" and "inspirational." Sam shrugged, thinking the whole thing couldn't be too tough. "Oh yeah. I got it."

"What about lunch?" Gabriel asked.

"Okay."

Gabriel looked at him for a moment. "What would you like?"

Sam shrugged. He felt his face warming. "I don't know . . . uh . . . mac and cheese?"

Gabriel smiled. "Seriously? From sushi and sirloin tips to mac and cheese?"

"I don't know. Sushi is good, too. Stop looking at me like that. Jeez. Who cares? It's lunch. PBJ. Hot dogs. Sushi. What-ever they have is fine." Sam wasn't acting because he truthfully didn't like Gabriel's squinty eyes glistening at him like a cat's.

Gabriel puckered his lips. "Whatever *you* want is what they'll have. *I'm* not the finicky eater. You are. You're the star, remember?"

"Well, I'm feeling easygoing today," Sam said. "And I've got a headache."

"Aspirin?" Gabriel reached into his shoulder bag and shook a couple out of a bottle.

"Thanks." Sam spoke quietly as he took them.

"And sushi for lunch."

"Fine."

"And radio satellite tour at twelve-thirty."

"Got it."

"Good, I'll be outside if you need me. I'll be back with lunch at noon. Meantime, I'll let you get some rest." Gabriel looked at the big overstuffed couch facing a huge plasma screen connected to an Xbox.

"Thanks."

Sam watched him go before flopping down on the couch to think.

39

SAM

It wasn't long before McKenna knocked. She let herself in before he could even answer and clapped the whole way across the room.

"You were fantastic! I couldn't believe it. I heard Pierce Everette gush about how great you are. How did you like it?"

"Honestly?" Sam said, sitting up. "It was awesome."

"See? I told you."

McKenna hugged him and Sam closed his eyes, breathing in the strawberry scent of her hair before she separated from him.

With wide eyes, she said, "Now let's call Stu. Let's get this script made into a movie. Can you imagine if we pulled that off? Are you ready? How fun is this?"

"Sure, we can call him now. How'd your scene go?"

"Oh, who cares. Fine, I guess. Blah blah blah. Stu's on your speed dial." McKenna nodded at the phone on the coffee table beside the Xbox controllers. "Number seven. Lucky."

Sam put a finger on the speed dial and recited his lines. "Hey, Stu, I've got this script you've got to see. You've got to help me get it made. I know you can do it. I want to help McKenna. She wants to play the girl. What do you think?"

"Perfect," McKenna said, "only don't ask him what he thinks. You don't care what he thinks. You tell him you want him to come over to the set. You want to give it to him *personally*—that's a big deal in Hollywood—and you want him to read it tonight."

"Tonight?"

"You're right. *Today.*"

"I thought he's a big agent. I can just tell him 'today'?"

"You're Trevor Goldman. Of course you can. And say it like you mean it."

Sam nodded and pressed the speed dial. Stu Lisson's assistant answered the phone. "Hello, Stu Lisson's office."

"Hi, it's . . . Trevor. Goldman. I need to talk to Stu."

"Hang on, Trevor."

Sam got put on hold. He gave McKenna a thumbs-up. It was less than a minute before the assistant got back on. "He'll be right with you."

Ten seconds later, Stu got on. "Trevooor. How's my franchise?"

"Hey, Stu. Great."

"You got a cold? You sound funny."

Sam cleared his throat. "A little. I'm okay."

"Attaboy. I heard *Bright Lights* knocked it out of the park with the focus groups. How's *Dragon's Empire*? You happy?

142

You got what you need? Dressing room with Xbox? Plenty of Skittles?"

"I'm great, Stu." Sam was blown away by his agent's enthusiastic kindness and felt funny making demands. "Um, I've got this script I really want you to look at. I *need* you to look at. Today. If you can."

McKenna shook her head violently and stabbed her finger at the floor.

"I want you to come here. Can you do it right now?"

Silence greeted Sam from the other end of the phone.

"I want to help McKenna." Sam spoke under his breath. "She loves it, too, and she wants to play the girl. It's called *Dark Cellar*."

"Oh, McKenna? You sly dog. I love it! Tell you what, I've got a lunch with those sharks from Universal so I'll swing by on my way out there. Good? By the way, what's *Dark Cellar*? A prison movie?"

"It's a horror flick. Old-school."

"Ah, the things we do for love. The things we do for love. I heard about your birthday present. Your father told me you loved it. How many kids get to knock it around with the big boys like that, huh? Wow. I can tell you, I remember when the Dodgers were in Brooklyn. Now *that* was baseball. Okay, I'll see you around twelve. I got Michael Eisner calling me. You good?"

"Good."

"Good."

Sam hung up, beaming. "I did it. I think I did it."

"Of course you did."

"McKenna? Want to sit down?"

They sat.

"McKenna, this is kind of crazy. I think I'm going to do it whether you think I should or not, but I want to tell you anyway."

"Tell me what?"

"McKenna, if Trevor and I are really twins . . ."

"Of course you are."

"Right, and we've got parents out there somewhere. Not, like, my dad or Trevor's mom, but whatever they call it. Birth parents or something."

"Biological parents." McKenna nodded.

"Well, I want to find our mother. I know it won't be easy. I mean, if I were just Sam Palomaki, I'm sure I couldn't. But I was thinking, as Trevor Goldman, especially if you help me, I mean, I've got money and people to do things and my dad is this powerful guy everyone's afraid of. I can *find* her, can't I?"

Sam watched McKenna think about it. She wrinkled her forehead, but then she smiled, and her smile grew. "I don't see why not."

"And you'll help me?" Sam asked.

"Absolutely."

40

TREVOR

Trevor hit it.

Not out of the park, not even through a hole. Actually, it went right down the first-base line so that Frankie Schmelling scooped it up and put him out. But that didn't matter. He hit it, and he *saw* it. He saw the red dot.

He started back toward the plate, trying not to grin, since Coach Sharp still wasn't very happy. He scooped up his bat and stepped up again.

The next pitch was a fastball. Trevor wasn't confused, and he blasted it, picking up a double, then jogging back to the plate.

Graham threw a curve, and this time Trevor got it, popping it over the second baseman and into the hole between right and center, a single. He jogged back again.

"What's the score, Coach?"

Coach Sharp looked down at his notepad. "You're behind RJ by eight points. You'd have to hit two more singles and a home run to even think about winning the M&M's."

"Nice."

Trevor felt a new joy, the return of confidence. Learning something, seeing it, and actually being able to make it happen. He hit two more singles, a home run, and a double.

"I love M&M's, Coach. Feeling better now. Must have been that pitch that hit me in the back. Got my timing off." Trevor rubbed the spot where Klum had nailed him, and it really was sore.

As it turned out, Trevor didn't win the candy. RJ had a big round, and no one was able to pass him. Still, Trevor came in second, which left him swelling with pride.

"Okay, guys," Coach Sharp said as the team gathered around him in a tight group on the grass, "not a bad practice, but we'll have to do better tomorrow. This team from Palos Verdes is good. They're not the best, but they're good, and we can't be sloppy. So, make sure you get some rest tonight. Get plenty of water because it looks like it'll be hot. Then get here early, say, eight, because I want to do an hour of batting before we drive to the game. We good? Okay, bring it in."

The team held up their hands and chanted "Champions!" together.

On the way to the parking lot, Trevor walked with Cole Price and the Schmelling brothers. They teased him about getting hit by Klum and Trevor just grinned, knowing it was all in fun.

"I thought you were smarter than that, razzing Klum and

asking for a beanball," RJ said.

"Yeah, after what happened to Brian Leonard, you go and try to hit him?" Frankie said.

"I thought he was going to rearrange your face," Cole said.

"Yeah, then maybe he wouldn't look like such a *movie star*." RJ batted his eyelids like a girl.

"Oh," Frankie said in a high-pitched voice, "I'm so pretty. Look at me. Just a touch of makeup and I'm ready for my close-up. I want to finish up so I can get to my dancing lessons."

The boys laughed, and Trevor felt his face get warm. "What's wrong with dancing?"

The three boys stopped and stared hard at him. Then, all at once, they burst out laughing and patted Trevor on the shoulder.

"What's wrong with dancing?" Frankie kept talking like a girl.

"Yes, I love to dance," Cole said, also in a high voice.

Trevor did his best to control his facial expressions. He thought of McKenna when she stuck two fingers up her nose and crossed her eyes behind Pierce Everette's back and he broke out into a grin, acting. They all had a good laugh, and Trevor knew he was back in the groove with Sam's teammates.

"You know," Trevor said. "It's gonna be different around here from now on."

"How so?" Frankie asked.

"Klum, that's how."

"Klum?" RJ stopped walking.

Trevor got excited. He knew all about bullies from the books he read and the movies he'd acted in. He knew the secret was to be tough right back to them and they'd crumble like cupcakes. All you had to have was confidence, and that's one thing Trevor had plenty of. "Him pushing us around? It's over."

"Over?" Cole said. "How?"

"Because I say so, that's how." Trevor let his acting slip away. He wanted to say a few things that fit *his* character, and not necessarily Sam's.

"Saying so won't be enough," Frankie said. "You know that."

"Then I'll *do* something." Trevor kept walking, and the group kept up with him. "In fact, next time I see that mope, I'm gonna bust him right in the mouth."

"Oh yeah? I'd pay money to see *that*." The voice came from behind Trevor and his little group, but when he turned around, it was clear that Scotty Needum had been skulking along behind them, listening in.

41
TREVOR

The look of shock and fear on the faces of Sam's friends was more disturbing to Trevor than the sight of Scotty Needum's pudgy face gone red with anger.

Trevor kept his chin up. "You want to see? Just show up early before the game tomorrow, and tell your punk friend to meet me behind the bathrooms over there."

Needum looked back at the low cinder-block building that stood just beyond the stands on the far side of the field. When he looked back at Trevor, his grin showed off two sharp incisor teeth on either side of his mouth.

"You're calling out Dorian?" Needum laughed so hard his belly jiggled. "Oh boy. I can't wait. You're dead. You are so dead."

The boys watched as Scotty Needum rumbled off to the parking lot, got into his mom's pickup, and drove away.

"Fine," Trevor said, but it didn't come out as strong as he

would have liked, and Sam's friends could only shake their heads as they walked away.

"You have to stand up to him." Trevor spoke to them in shouts as they got into their respective cars. "He's a bully! Watch and see what happens! Don't be chickens!"

Trevor watched them all go before he climbed into the old beat-up Ferrari Sam's dad drove up in.

"Good practice?" Sam's dad asked.

"Not bad," Trevor said.

"What were you shouting to those guys about?" Sam's dad asked as he backed out of his spot and spun around.

"I had some trouble hitting Graham's curveball; I was telling them not to worry about it."

"Graham? I thought he was almost afraid to pitch to you."

"Well, I lost my confidence, I guess, hitting that curveball of his. I got it back, though."

"'Our doubts are traitors, and make us lose the good we oft might win.'" Sam's dad glanced over at Trevor as he pulled out onto the highway.

"Uh, *Othello*?"

"*Othello*? Come on, Sam. *Measure for Measure*."

Trevor hit his own forehead. "Oh yeah. Of course. I got hit by a pitch."

"In the head?" Sam's dad scowled and glanced at Trevor again.

"No, no. In the back. I spun around. Klum threw for my head, though. Coach kicked him out of practice."

Sam's dad gripped the wheel until his knuckles turned white. "You know I don't like to talk bad about anyone, Sam, and you shouldn't either, but I swear that kid is a bad egg. He's a *rotten* egg. Rotten as the state of Denmark. I have to say it."

"'Something is rotten in the State of Denmark.' *Hamlet*." Trevor grinned with pride at recognizing the Shakespeare quote.

"Ha! Yes. Well done."

They rode for a few minutes in silence, and Trevor wondered what Sam's dad was thinking. He wanted to ask, but didn't know if it was something Sam would do or not, so he kept quiet.

"So, you're not going to ask about the surprise?" Sam's dad asked.

With everything else to think about, Trevor had forgotten all about it.

"Sure," he said, "what's the surprise?"

42

SAM

Stu was the key.

That's what McKenna said, and Sam had to go with what she said. Without her, he was blind, deaf, and dumb. She said Stu knew everything and had seen everything.

"They said he was the one who lined up the detective agency that caught Brad Pitt with Angelina when he was still married to Jennifer Aniston," McKenna said, "so you know he's got the connections. Get him to take care of the script first, then you spring it on him. All he has to do is give you a name. We can take care of the rest."

So, they had lunch and played Nazi Zombies until Gabriel knocked on the dressing room door to announce that Stu had arrived and remind Sam about the radio interviews.

Sam could hear the loud agent outside the dressing room

talking in a shout to the director, telling him how great he was. Even in just the few hours he'd been exposed to this life, Sam already knew that everyone said everything was "great." Nothing was ever bad. No one was unhappy. You just didn't frown, not in public anyway.

"Boychik!" Stu barged in wearing a dark pinstripe suit with a tie so red it made Sam blink. "You're the greatest. The biggest star in my galaxy. I said to Tom Hanks just the other day, I said, 'Tommy, you've been eclipsed. Trevor Goldman is outshining everyone.' You know what he said? He said, 'You tell Trevor he messed in his diaper on the set of *Bombshell*.' You remember that flick?"

Sam just stared. He had never heard of it.

"Right, everyone tries to forget that one. Ha-ha! Look at you. You need to eat. I tell you that all the time and I sound like my bubby, I know, but I can't help myself. Eat. Eat. Eat."

Stu seemed to catch his breath as he looked around the room. "Good. Skittles like you like, purple and red only. Xbox. The beautiful costar. Ahhh."

Stu clucked his tongue, scolding Sam. Sam's face burned, and he looked away from McKenna.

"So," Stu said, "let's talk business. This script . . ."

"I want you to read it." Sam lifted it off the coffee table, handing it to Stu.

"Sounds like it inspired you." Stu turned to McKenna. "And *you*, right? It inspired you? You want to play something in this?"

"I love old-school horror," McKenna said.

"*Texas Chainsaw Massacre, Friday the 13th,* that kind of stuff," Sam said.

McKenna nodded. "The father in *Dark Cellar* has a girl my age. It is so good, and scary."

Stu hefted the manuscript and flipped through the first couple pages. "Okay. Okay, I see where it's going. Not bad. Could use a punch-up, but obviously a solid writer. Never heard of this guy, though. Randall Palomaki?"

"So, we discover him," Sam said.

Stu looked at him.

"*You* discover him," Sam said.

Stu smiled. "That's my job. Okay, I'll read it. You had me at 'hello' kid, you know that. Let me give you my read, then I'll talk to your dad."

"My dad?" Sam said, deciding he had nothing to lose. "Come on, Stu. I'm not messing my diaper on the set with Tom Hanks. Give me a little more credit. You don't have go to my dad for everything, do you?"

"What, you want me to peddle this around without telling your dad?" Stu's smile turned into a chuckle.

"Why not?" Sam said.

Stu stared for a minute, then burst out laughing. "Right, why not? What? Do I look drunk to you? Not loop in your dad? You know who didn't loop in your dad? Myron Kettle."

"Who's Myron Kettle?" Sam asked.

"Exactly," Stu said. "Myron Kettle is no one. He *woulda* been a player in this town, but he didn't loop your dad into something your dad wanted to be looped into."

Stu slapped his hands together as if he were knocking off

some dust. "And *that*, I don't do. You want to be a rebel without a cause? Wait a couple years. Get a tattoo or pierce your nose or something. That'll teach the old man. But in the meantime, don't expect me or anyone with their brains planted firmly in their heads to risk their gullets by not looping in your dad."

Stu let the script fall to the coffee table with a thud. "It's just not done."

43

TREVOR

"Disneyland!" Sam's dad held up two tickets. "How about that? I got them for a door prize at the Save the Oceans fundraiser. Never told you. Wanted to surprise you. California Screamin'? Tower of Terror? You ready?"

"Uh, sure."

"Uh, sure? You've been screamin' for California Screamin' for two years."

Trevor opened his mouth to say that he'd been on California Screamin' so many times he never cared if he saw it again. Three times he'd been to private parties that they'd closed the park for, and even though the rides were fun, what Trevor really wanted to do was hit baseballs—curveballs to be specific.

"Dad, if you don't mind, could we just go to the batting cage?"

"What?" Sam's dad glanced at him in disbelief and the car

seemed to slow down. "You're playing with me, right?"

"I just want to make sure I've got my groove for the game tomorrow. I told you, today I was a little off."

"You have to take time and have fun, too, Sam."

"Hitting is fun," Trevor said.

Sam's dad nodded, but Trevor knew he'd disappointed the man. Still, he didn't know how long he'd get to pinch-hit for Sam, and if he only got to play in one game, he sure wanted to make it a good one. If it were his own father, Trevor knew the day would now be ruined. People didn't often change his father's plans, and if they ever did, things didn't go well. So, Trevor was surprised to see Sam's dad brighten up and actually start to whistle as he pulled off the highway and into a huge batting cage facility with a long row of cages curving around a central cluster of machines. Above, a black web of netting hung from several tall poles.

"You're right, Sam," Sam's dad said as he cut the engine. "I admire your discipline. You know what you want, and you're going to get it. You're not afraid to work for it, either, to sacrifice. 'Perseverance, dear my lord, keeps honor bright.'"

"No idea," Sam said, knowing he was expected to guess which of Shakespeare's plays the quote was from.

"*Troilus and Cressida.*"

"Right."

"I'll get some tokens and meet you in the cage."

Trevor nodded, removed his bat bag from behind the seat, and trudged toward the dusty cages in the heat. The thump of bats on rubber balls and hissing spit of machines used by other customers filled the air. While Sam's dad was buying tokens,

Trevor examined the coin box and saw that with a simple switch he could choose to have curveballs thrown at him. When Sam's dad returned with a handful of tokens, Trevor fed the machine and got into position with his bat. The machine whirred and spit out a curveball.

Trevor swung and missed, but realized what he did. The yellow rubber balls didn't show a red dot, and that slightest instant of confusion kept him from connecting. He took a breath, because he didn't need to read these pitches; he knew they'd be curves. He just needed to work on the mechanics of hitting a curve. Reading the pitch would require a real leather ball in the machine, or an actual pitcher to throw to him.

If he was in his old life, either one would be easy. He could send someone out to get white leather balls with red laces to feed into his own machine, or he could hire a retired pro player to throw curveballs to him in his backyard. But as Sam Palomaki, he'd have to make do with what he had, and right now, that was just a dirty batting cage with grimy rubber balls.

He focused on keeping his weight back and tightened his muscles for a quick swing. The second pitch came. He swung, and connected.

Sam's dad sat outside the cage on a metal bench. "That didn't look off at all, nice contact."

Trevor nodded and kept swinging, gaining more and more confidence as he went. By the time he'd used up all his tokens, Trevor had a nice sweat going. Between the batting cage and the practice before, his arms were tired, and he was ready for a break.

"How about lunch?" Sam's dad said.

"And then can we come back later?" Trevor asked.

Sam's dad hesitated. "You don't think that'd be overdoing it?"

Trevor rotated his arms, working out the fatigue. "After a rest I should be okay."

Sam's dad shrugged. "In and Out?"

"Good by me."

They got back onto the highway and went to the next exit where the In and Out Burger was. Sam's dad wanted to talk about his script and some meetings he had set up next week that he was excited about. It took all of Trevor's concentration to fake some enthusiasm, since he knew the best chance Sam's dad would ever have was through him and McKenna.

Still, he kept it up. After lunch, they returned to the batting cage. Sam's dad bought another handful of tokens and sat on the bench while Trevor went at it again. His determination paid off because by the last set of pitches he was actually able to give some direction to his hits, pulling them toward third or pushing them toward first by swinging a bit sooner or later. So he was feeling really good when he heard a cell phone ring and Sam's dad answer it. Without trying to listen, he heard Sam's dad talk and the name Klum jumped out at him.

"Mr. Klum, hello . . . Okay, Doug, sure . . . Right, Sam told me he got hit. . . . I did know that. . . . What? That doesn't sound like Sam to me. . . . No, I'm not saying that, but . . . Of course we'll sit down to clear the air. . . . Well, we're just finishing up at the batting cages. . . . They do work hard, don't they? Yes . . . We had lunch already, thanks, but how about the Jamba Juice over on Eagle Rock Boulevard? . . . Sure, fifteen minutes is fine. . . . No, I agree. See you then."

Trevor stared at Sam's dad through the cage. "What was that?"

Sam's dad scowled. "Sam, did you threaten to fight the Klum kid?"

Trevor's mouth went slack, because he wasn't sure exactly what he should say.

"Doug Klum says you did, and that a bunch of your teammates heard you say it."

Trevor thought of Scotty Needum's fat red face, and he clenched his teeth. "That kid hit me with a pitch, on purpose!"

"But *fighting*? That's not part of the game." Sam's dad scowled.

Trevor wanted to swing his bat into the fence. His palms began to sweat.

"He's a jerk."

"I know that, but I've taught you that fighting is never the answer for a problem." Sam's dad shook his head. "I just hope you didn't cost yourself a spot on the team."

Trevor's insides collapsed into mush. "You mean, not play tomorrow?"

"Tomorrow? Son, if you think you can go around threatening your teammates to fights behind the bathrooms before a big game, you may have cost yourself a spot on the Blue Sox *for good*."

44

SAM

Stu scooped a handful of Skittles out of the bowl on the table and filled his mouth, chewing loudly and speaking fast at the same time. "Coulda saved me a trip. Not that it wasn't good to see you. See that set out there. Pierce Everette. I tell you, I remember when he was shagging coffee and splicing film together for Maury Rappaport at MGM, and look at him now. I heard the number on this flick is north of a hundred million."

"Stu," McKenna said, "I get it that Trevor's dad might want to know what you were doing with a script that came from Trevor, because a lot of people would think he was the one really behind it, so he'd want to know. But what if the script didn't come from Trevor? What if this came from *me*?"

Stu scratched the back of his neck and looked around. "You guys . . . You're what, kids? Aren't you supposed to be playing with jacks or jump ropes or something?"

McKenna stood, picked up the manuscript off the coffee table, and held it out to Stu. "Stu, would you mind looking at this for me. I'd like to play the role of the daughter. If you like it, would you shop it around for me? Maybe get an auction going?"

Stu's eyes went from Sam to McKenna and back to Sam.

Sam played his part. "I'm really behind this, Stu. The script McKenna gave to you. I'd like to see it get done. I won't forget the favor, either."

"And, you want to see it happen because you like McKenna." Stu spoke slowly, as if explaining it to himself. "You two are good friends. It's her script, though. Her idea."

"That's right. This is all about McKenna. I'm just support-ing *her*." Sam was beginning to get a sense of just how powerful, and feared, Trevor's dad really was.

"You're a nice kid like that." Stu slowly tucked the script under his arm and scooped up more Skittles. "I think I'm see-ing it."

"Great," Sam said, feeling back on track and ready to move on. "So, there's one more thing I need your help at."

"One more thing?" The clump of half-chewed Skittles rolled into the front of Stu's mouth before he tilted his head back to get it under control. "Somethin' easy, right?"

"I don't know how hard it will be." Sam spoke softly, but with an urgency that caused Stu and McKenna to lean toward him. "Maybe easy, maybe more. I don't want you to do any-thing, Stu. Just get me the right person."

162

"Person for what?" Stu swallowed and lowered his voice as well.

"To help me find my biological mom."

"Your mom, as in the woman who gave birth to you? As in the woman who *isn't* Diana Goldman?"

Stu blinked at him, returned the script to the coffee table, then sat down on the couch and rested a gentle hand on Sam's knee. "Trevor. First thing is: I never heard whatever it was you said to me just now. Second, you may as well never mention it to anyone ever again, because if your dad found out—and the man has a strange way of finding out just about everything, trust me—he would never allow it.

"Not ever."

45
SAM

"But why?" Sam asked.

"Why is the sky blue and the sun yellow?" Stu got up, tucked the script under his arm again, and gave it a pat. "McKenna, you can count on me. You know that. This I can do. How about I read *Dark Cellar* and let you know?"

"Today?" Sam said.

Stu turned. "You feeling okay? 'Cause if I didn't know better, I'd say you're coming down with something. You're not yourself. Still, I can get it done. What your hurry is, I can't tell, because we all know these things take time."

"Sometimes they happen quick, though," McKenna said.

The hope in her voice made Sam like her even more, if that were possible.

"You never know," McKenna said suddenly. "If it can happen quick, it'll happen with Stu. That much we know."

Sam turned to Stu. "Are you sure you can't help me find—"

"Hey! Hey!" Stu held up his hand like a traffic cop, speaking in rapid bursts. "Didn't hear it. Won't hear it. Use your head. Nothing good can ever come from *that* soap opera, and that's just your dad. We didn't even mention how your mom would react. Can you even imagine those fireworks?"

McKenna waved a hand, signaling Sam to let it go, so he dropped it, thanking Stu along with her and repeating how much he wanted to see "McKenna's" script get all the way to a green light.

"Green lights are what I do." Stu walked out, then poked his head back around the corner. "They call me Mr. Greenlight. Did I ever tell you that? No? They do."

Then he was gone.

"Wow," Sam said. "Guy's like a Super Ball in a coat closet."

"That's a real agent for you."

"Are they all like Stu?" Sam asked.

"Maybe *like* him, but there's only one Stu. That, I promise you."

Sam scooped up a handful of Skittles and let them drain through his fingers back into the bowl. "So, what do we do now?"

"Now, we wait. What you said was perfect. He'll read the script and he'll like it. He'll attach me to it and get some other actors, too, maybe a director."

"No," Sam said, "I don't mean the script. I'm talking about my biological mom. I thought you said Stu would help."

"I thought so, but I guess I see his point." McKenna flopped down on the couch. "If he helped and your—I mean, Trevor's—parents found out, it sounds like they wouldn't be too happy."

165

"So what am I supposed to do, just give up?"

"How bad do you want to find her, your mother?"

Sam shrugged. It was a door he had never opened before in his life. He never thought about family beyond his own dad and the mom he never really knew. But now that the door was opened, he felt an unexplainable, burning need to go through it and have a mom to make proud. He wanted see where he'd come from, *who* he'd come from. And there was also something else, deep and dark. Sam wanted to know why. Why would his mom have given him and Trevor away?

"Pretty bad, I guess," he said.

"Good." McKenna nodded and spoke in a low voice. "Because this could be risky, but there is someone else I know who's good at finding out things who I think would help us."

Sam asked, "Who?"

46

TREVOR

Trevor swallowed down the acid bubbling up from his stomach. "Dad, I just wanted him to stop bullying me and the rest of the guys."

"Stopping a bully by becoming one yourself? Fighting?" Sam's dad shook his head. "I taught you better than that. Does this have anything to do with that McKenna Steele and your haircut."

"No." Trevor shook his head violently.

"Because you haven't been yourself, that's for sure, and I have a pretty strong feeling that something's going on."

"What could go on?" Trevor fought hard to keep the panic out of his voice.

Sam's dad stared at him through the fence. Finally, he said, "Okay, if you want to play it that way. Come on. Let's go meet the Klums."

Trevor followed Sam's dad to the car. Fifteen minutes later

they pulled into a small strip mall and stopped in front of the Jamba Juice. Trevor had had plenty of Jamba Juice over the years, but he'd never gone to a store for one. It was always a production assistant, or PA, who would take orders from people on the set, especially the stars and the director, and go out to buy the juice or coffee, or whatever anyone wanted. Trevor was curious, and almost excited to be doing something that any normal person could do. Whatever excitement he had went out the door when he saw Dorian Klum and his father sitting at the table just inside the window.

Part of Trevor wanted to march in there and give the Klums a piece of his mind. No one would mess with Trevor Goldman like that, and he didn't see why Sam had to put up with it either. But Trevor knew better than to ruin things for Sam, so he quickly put the script together in his mind and decided on the expressions of regret and humility that he'd have to paste across his face. Sam's dad held the door for him, but he let Sam's dad take the lead on approaching the table.

Sam's dad shook hands with both of the Klums. Trevor did the same, and they all sat down. Mr. Klum was a heavy mountain of a man with a shaved tan head and a small gold hoop in one ear. Without his striped blue-and-white golf shirt and khaki shorts, he would have been a perfect pirate, and Trevor suspected he knew where Dorian got not only his size, but also his meanness. Mr. Klum's voice, however, was a surprise. He spoke with a southern accent in a pitch nearly as high as a woman's, and he smiled politely as he said, "I'm Doug. Thanks for coming, Randall. Is it okay if I call you Randall?"

"Of course," Sam's dad said.

"And Sam, I want to thank you, and I like your haircut, son." The big man looked at Trevor with eyes that glinted like small blue marbles. "Now, I know both you boys have your eyes on that USC Elite Training Center, and I know they only take one, so it's understandable that you've set yourselves up as rivals, even though you're on the same team. So, I think both Randall and I realize that with kids like you and Dorian—both fierce competitors, both shooting for the same thing—there's gonna be friction between you. That's natural, and there isn't any sense in pretending otherwise.

"But still, what's happening now just isn't right."

Dorian nodded smugly.

"And that's you, too, Dorian," Mr. Klum said with a flash of that angry pirate Trevor knew he could become.

Dorian's face went blank.

"Because you hit him with a pitch," Mr. Klum said.

"By accident!" Dorian burst like a shaken soda bottle.

"Okay." Mr. Klum held up his hand and spoke calmly. "Let's say it was by accident. But Sam didn't *think* it was an accident, and so Sam wants to get you back."

"Which *he* knows better than." Sam's dad cast a scowl at Trevor.

"Well," Mr. Klum said. "We think Dorian owes Sam an apology and an explanation, and then maybe Sam won't feel so strongly about it."

"And Sam owes Dorian an apology along with the assurance that this fighting business is never going to happen again, no matter what happens on the practice field. Right, Sam?" Sam's father turned to him, waiting for a yes.

47

TREVOR

Trevor nodded and let his chin sag, looking at the table. "Yes."

"Yes, and?" Sam's father said.

Trevor looked up at Dorian Klum with a mask of humility and took a deep breath to deliver his lines. "Dorian, I'm sorry. I shouldn't have talked about fighting you. We're teammates, and we need each other. It won't happen again, and I want to wish you good luck with USC Elite. Let's just play to win and whoever gets lucky gets to go. If it's you, then it's because you deserve it."

A glimmer of delight danced across Dorian Klum's eyes. "And I'm sorry about hitting you with the pitch, Sam. I honestly had no intention of hitting you. I would never do that."

Trevor was nearly bursting with the urge to shout out Brian Leonard's name, but he kept quiet and nodded instead.

"It's just that sometimes I get excited and throw wild pitches.

I try not to, but . . . I don't know, sometimes it just happens."
Dorian looked at his father, who nodded with satisfaction.

Dorian scooped up his Jamba Juice smoothie and sucked down the last bit until it made slurping noises. Trevor looked at Sam's dad.

"Well," Sam's dad said, "this sounds great. I'm really glad you called me, Doug."

"I am, too." Mr. Klum waved his head toward the counter. "Randall, I'm going to get us another round; why don't you get one for you and Sam? Dorian, another blackberry?"

Sam's dad hesitated, but Mr. Klum narrowed his eyes with a knowing expression and nodded his head to encourage Sam's dad to go along.

"Sure," Sam's dad said. "Mango, Sam?"

Trevor nodded.

"I'll have banana, Dad," Dorian said.

Mr. Klum whispered to Sam's dad as they walked away. Trevor thought he heard the words "Good for them to be alone." He turned his attention back to Dorian, who continued to slurp his smoothie as his eyes followed the two fathers.

As soon as they were out of earshot, Dorian slapped his cup down and leaned across the table. His mouth curled into a snarl, and his eyes kept darting toward the counter to make sure he couldn't be heard. "Just so you know, *punk*, *I* didn't tell. If Scotty Needum wasn't an *idiot*, you and I would be on. That rock head talked about you wanting to fight on speakerphone. That's the first thing."

Trevor swallowed back some nasty words of his own, but he let his hatred for Klum flood his eyes.

Klum clenched his jaw so hard it shook before he opened his mouth again. "Second thing is this: I so bad want to beat you into pulp. *So bad*. My knuckles are aching. And when this is over, that's exactly what I'm going to do and I want you to know it and think about how it's going to *feel* to have your teeth kicked into the back of your head."

Dorian's eyes flickered back toward the counter.

"And one more thing, you goofy, shaved-headed freak, there is no way in the world you're going to beat me to USC Elite. I am so much better than you that it hurts. I'm gonna stomp you like a roach. I threw that pitch at your *face*, and the only thing I'm sorry about is that you spun around like a little ballerina and I missed. But don't think I won't try it again."

Klum shook his head and dropped his voice into a crazy, hateful whisper. "Don't think that *at all*."

48
SAM

Before McKenna could answer Sam, Gabriel knocked and came in, carrying a cell phone. "Ready for the radio interviews? You want me to attach a headset?"

Gabriel held up an earpiece connected to a thin microphone on a flexible wire.

"Sure." Sam took the headset and put it on. Gabriel dialed a number. Sam sat on the couch and picked up the sheet of publicity notes.

"I'll be back," McKenna said, ducking out.

Sam watched her go. Gabriel sat down next to him and crossed his legs.

"Why are you looking at me like that?" Sam said.

"Like what?" Gabriel was smiling like a cat, and something told Sam that he *knew*.

Sam shrugged and, before he could find the words, a pleasant woman answered the phone.

"Hi, Trevor. I'm Laurie Warren. I'll be directing your satellite tour today and for the next few days. I'll keep things moving so they don't overlap into each other. You know how it goes; you give them three minutes and they want ten."

Sam watched Gabriel walk out. He looked carefully at the list, and his mouth went dry. First up was a taped segment with Ryan Seacrest. The famous radio host asked Sam about the movie and Sam literally read from the studio's page of notes, stumbling and bumbling.

Seacrest laughed. "You're kidding me, right, Trevor? Did you have some dental work done this morning and the gas hasn't worn off?"

Sam didn't know what to do. "Sorry, Mr. Seacrest. I'm not feeling too great. Sorry."

"Oh." Seacrest's voice softened a bit. "I guess even a star has an off day, right, Trevor?"

Sam forced a small laugh.

"But we know *Bright Lights* is going to be a big hit, so we'll all get out and see it, buddy. Good luck with *Dragon's Empire* and we'll talk to you again soon."

Before Sam could catch his breath, Laurie Warren jumped back on the line and said, "Liane Hansen from NPR's *Weekend Edition*."

Sam did better with the NPR host, and better with the next interview after that. By the time he'd finished, Sam felt like he was a pro. He wondered what Gabriel was up to, but as he went to open the dressing room door, it opened and McKenna spilled inside.

"Oh good," she said, "you're done. I got her. She's in and she's got the right person! Sam, this is so great. We're going to find your mother!"

"Wait." Sam lowered his voice and ushered McKenna to the couch. "You didn't even tell me who she is."

"Sara, of course."

"Sara Grant? Your publicist?"

"She knows a lot of people, and she knew just who to call. Remember *California Private Eyes*?"

"The TV show?"

"Yeah," McKenna said. "Remember the guy with the handlebar mustache?"

"The bald guy?"

"Yeah, Dale Moffit. Well, the show got canceled, but he's the real deal. He just went back to his old job. Sara knew him because she represented him. He even spied on her husband when they got divorced."

"Great." Sam rolled his eyes.

"That's what private investigators do." McKenna pouted at him. "You think there's a world of rich kids looking for their biological moms? Everybody gets divorced, so that's where the market is. It's all the same, finding people and following them. Stop being so ungrateful, will you?"

"Sorry." Sam sat down and offered her the bowl of Skittles. "I'm jumpy is all. I blew the interview with Ryan Seacrest and told him I was feeling sick, and Gabriel keeps looking at me funny. I swear, I think he knows."

McKenna took a Skittle and popped it in her mouth, chewing while she talked. "Gabriel? He's paid not to know. Even if he knew, he'd keep quiet because think about how bad it makes him look. Your dad—Trevor's dad, I mean—would go ballistic if he knew Trevor bailed on the set and is running around playing baseball, and Gabriel would get the brunt of it."

"But Gabriel didn't do anything. Me and Trevor did . . . and you."

McKenna smiled. "But that's not how this town works. If you're a star, you're above it. If you're not, you take the fall. It's like the whipping boys they used to have for the princes back in medieval times. You know what a whipping boy is?"

Sam shook his head.

"If the prince did something wrong, no one could punish him. He was the prince. Still, someone had to be punished, so they'd have a whipping boy. Some poor schlep who got whipped whenever the prince did something wrong."

"That's the stupidest thing ever," Sam said.

"Maybe that's why it was called the Dark Ages." McKenna took another Skittle. "Anyway, Dale Moffit is already on it."

"How do we pay him?" Sam asked.

"Pay him? You're Trevor Goldman. You know how many people want to do favors for you? He doesn't want money. He's thrilled to do it."

Sam shook his head in disbelief. "You're like a genie in a bottle. I want my dad's script made, *poof*, you got Stu working on it. I want to find my mom, *poof*, you got a private investigator in full swing."

McKenna stared at him, then reached out and touched his shoulder. "It's not magic, Sam. Trevor Goldman is a star with a movie star mom and a dad who's one of the top five most powerful people in Hollywood. He gets what he wants, when he wants it."

Sam shook his head. "But I'm not him."

"To everyone else you are. Nice, isn't it?"

"Last night I wanted to switch back."

"And now?" McKenna asked.

"Riding around in a limousine? My own batting cage? Everybody hopping to get whatever I want? I could get used to this."

"I know. It's fun, right? The only thing you do have to do is remember Moffit, that's all. You owe him a favor. Come on, you gotta start getting ready for the next scene. I'll let Gabriel know to tell makeup."

"Well, how's Trevor going to feel owing a favor?" Sam went over to the mirror and sat down.

McKenna opened the door and spoke to Gabriel, then she appeared in the mirror over Sam's shoulder. "Trevor will be fine. This whole thing was his idea to begin with, right? And I gotta believe he's going to want to find your mom just as bad as you do.

"Why wouldn't he?"

49

TREVOR

Trevor opened his mouth, unable to hold back anymore. He let his face twist with rage. "You're junk, just rotten, stinky *junk*."

Laughter made Trevor turn his head. The two fathers had four cups of juice and were getting along just fine.

Sam's dad gave Trevor a worried look. "What are you guys talking about?"

Trevor forced his face into a smile. "Just how bad we're going to beat Palos Verdes and how their pitching is junk."

"Oh." Sam's dad looked relieved as he set a mango smoothie in front of Trevor. "Good."

Trevor pretended to sip the smoothie, but had no interest in drinking since the sight of Dorian Klum's smiling face made him want to vomit. The two fathers talked like old friends about the Dodgers, and they both agreed with the predictions that this was going to be their year to win it all. Trevor used the meditation techniques he'd learned from Margie Haber's private acting lessons to ignore Klum and actually remove himself mentally from the situation.

Sam's dad startled Trevor when he touched his arm. "Right, Sam?"

"Oh yeah. Right." Trevor blinked at Sam's dad and let his eyes sweep right past Dorian Klum.

Mr. Klum checked his watch. "So, I guess we better be going."

Trevor popped up out of his seat, extending a hand to the older Klum. Sam's dad nodded with approval. Trevor shook Dorian's hand, too.

"See you tomorrow, Dorian," Trevor said, forcing a smile.

Dorian smirked. "Yeah, see you, buddy."

"See? This is great. Thanks, guys," Mr. Klum said.

Trevor couldn't get out of there fast enough, but he forced himself to walk slowly. Inside the Ferrari, Sam's dad praised him. "It feels good to do the right thing, doesn't it?"

"Yes." Trevor forced himself to keep his eye on the prize: playing tomorrow. He so badly wanted to tell Sam's dad what a real jerk Dorian Klum was, but to do so would only jeopardize things. It was easier to let it slide, but he also felt bad for Sam that he'd have to put up with the fallout from Trevor's challenge to a fight. He made a mental note to tell Sam all about it and apologize whenever they spoke. That thought brought him to Sam, the text message he sent during practice that morning, and the idea of finding their biological parents.

"What's the matter?" Sam's dad asked him. "The smell making you a little queasy? Roll up your window. I'll put on the AC."

Trevor did smell the garbage cooking in the late afternoon

179

sunshine. Sam's dad turned a bend that Trevor recognized as the last turn before the trailer.

"No," Trevor said. "I'm fine."

"Sometimes the stink gets me when I've been away all day." Sam's dad put the sun visor down and returned his hands to the wheel, keeping his voice as cheerful as the smile on his face. "But it goes away in about twenty minutes. That's not too bad to put up with. I mean, how many people live this close to LA and don't have other people living on top of them? Life is all about trade-offs, Sam. You know I always say that."

Trevor only nodded and schemed about how he might sneak away to make a call to Sam. He needed to *talk* to his newfound brother, not just text him. He needed to tell Sam that no way should he try to find their biological parents. Trevor knew instinctively that something like that would be a disaster, maybe not for Sam, but for him. He was famous. His family was rich. As much as Trevor might like to satisfy the curiosity he felt, he knew better than open a door that he'd never be able to close.

He couldn't imagine how far Sam had progressed with this wild idea, but if McKenna was involved, the answer was pretty far.

The car stopped and Trevor hopped out, gripping Sam's phone in his pocket.

"Where you going?" Sam's dad asked.

"Just a walk," Trevor said, his feet kicking up dust along the tracks they'd just made.

"A walk?"

Trevor knew by the sound of Sam's dad's voice that a walk

wasn't something Sam just did, but he didn't care. The thought that Sam and McKenna had made progress on what he knew would be a disaster suddenly filled him with dread.

"I'll be back," he said over his shoulder.

Trevor kept going, looking back to see Sam's dad shrug and step up into the trailer. Then Trevor whipped out the phone and dialed, determined to stop Sam, no matter where he was in his search, no matter what the cost.

Sam shot three more scenes, banging out his simple lines like he'd been born to do it. He changed back into jeans and his T-shirt, then got into the back of the limo with Gabriel. He hated saying good-bye to McKenna, not just because he felt naked without her to advise him on things, but because when he drove away with her waving from outside the soundstage, he felt like a piece of him had gone missing. It was strange, as if he were a Swiss watch, still running, but missing a tiny flywheel that kept everything else in rhythm.

Sam sighed and thought about texting her. Gabriel was busy sending emails on his BlackBerry. Dolph grinned at him in the rearview mirror, held up the jersey, and gave Sam a thumbs-up. Sam also saw that he'd put a muzzle on Wolf. The dog simply stared at Sam with sad eyes and continued to whine, but much more quietly.

Sam smiled back at Dolph before letting his thoughts return to McKenna. Sam's palms began to sweat at the thought of what he wanted to say. He'd be going out on a limb if he did, so he considered several other things, things that would be much more bland, much more normal. If he texted her what he wanted and it backfired, he'd feel terrible. Maybe he should keep his thoughts to himself and just hope she'd reach out to him if she felt the same way.

The only thing that gave him hope was when she said she didn't think he should be Trevor, but rather just himself. Sam wasn't quite sure what that meant. Maybe it was the way everything seemed possible in the shoes of Trevor Goldman, but whatever the reason, Sam typed in the letters and sent the text, quickly, before snapping his phone shut and staring out the window.

Nothing happened. He waited, and glanced at Gabriel before he slowly opened the phone to make sure he'd really sent it and to reread the words he'd typed. He took a deep breath and opened the message to McKenna:

miss u already

He closed the phone a second time and stuffed it into the pocket of his jeans. When it buzzed, he nearly jumped out of his seat.

51

SAM

The buzzing wasn't a text; it was a call.

It wasn't McKenna.

It was Trevor.

Sam glanced at Gabriel, who looked up and smiled at him. Sam hit Ignore on the phone and replaced it in his pocket.

The phone buzzed again. Sam checked it, saw it was Trevor, and ignored it again. Trevor kept calling.

Frustrated, Sam kept hitting Ignore, wondering why in the world Trevor wouldn't stop. He had to know that Sam might have people around him and that he couldn't just pick up the phone and start talking. That would be foolish.

Sam waited until the limousine pulled up into the grand estate before he jumped out.

"See you tomorrow, Gabriel," he said. Before Gabriel could reply, Sam slammed the door shut.

He headed immediately out toward the back of the garage. He was pretty sure there wouldn't be anyone around the batting cage. The phone rang again.

Sam snapped it open as he walked. Trevor shouted at him to pick up the phone when he called.

Sam ground his teeth. "Trevor, are you kidding me? I didn't answer for a reason. Gabriel was sitting right next to me. And by the way, you forgot to tell me about that little detail of riding around with a killer dog named Wolf, and you're mad at me? Are you serious?"

Silence greeted him for a moment, and Sam began to think he'd lost the connection before Trevor said, "I have to talk to you. You can't do it."

"Can't do what?" Sam was annoyed. "You should have seen me deliver those lines today. Pierce Everette kept calling me beautiful."

"I don't care about that. Our mother. Our biological mother. You can't do it, Sam."

"Why?"

Silence again. "Because it'll ruin my whole life, that's why."

"What are you talking about? How could that ruin your life? You get everything you want, when you want. Our biological mother is not going to be able to touch you if you don't want her to."

To Sam, it was a no-brainer.

"My parents, Sam. They're not like your dad. Everything people say, everything that's written and on TV, it *matters* to them. It's everything to them, especially my mom. That's their world. They don't even talk about me being adopted, and no

185

one ever mentions it to them, not ever. Trust me, they do not want her in my life, or in theirs. You can't just pop open that door and let her through."

It was Sam's turn to be silent for a moment. When he spoke, he hunched over the phone and spoke in an urgent whisper. "She's our mother, Trevor. Did you ever think about what that means? Maybe she has no idea what happened to us, even if we're alive or dead. Look at your life."

Sam looked past the batting cage, up at the enormous house and the trees and gardens surrounding it. "Don't you want her to know how good you've got it?"

"It's none of her business," Trevor said. "Don't you get it? She didn't want me. She didn't want me and she didn't want *you*."

Sam felt like he'd been punched in the gut by his deepest fear.

"Look, this wasn't part of the deal," Trevor said. "You never told me you were going to do something like this. This is . . . it's crazy, and it'll make a mess I don't want and you don't need. I want to play baseball, but if you think you can start changing the deal, I'll just drop the whole thing right now and switch back."

"Fine," Sam said.

"Good," Trevor said.

"Because I'm sure you must have looked pretty bad today at practice." Sam was steaming.

"Too bad no one knew the difference."

"Right, you had to ask how to hit a stinking curveball." Sam snorted.

"Because I never hit one until today," Trevor said, his voice rising. "But guess what? I hit it and then I went to the cage

186

and hit about two hundred of them and now I got it because it's *easy.* And, I also did what you should have done to Dorian Klum if you weren't such a chicken. The guy threw a beanball at me today—*thinking it was you*—and, unlike you, I didn't just take it."

"What? You *what*? What the heck are you doing? We were supposed to blend in, remember?"

"Blend in? Blend *in*?" Trevor laughed on the other end of the phone. "You call planning to find our biological mother *blending in*? My parents would go nuts. You could find some crackpot who just wants to get on the cover of *People* magazine."

Sam was so angry, he was nearly out of breath. "I guess if I grew up with a mother like yours, I might think that about our mother, too."

Trevor went silent.

Sam looked up at the house. He saw a gardener slip out of the roses and into the hedge beyond with a set of hand shears. Trevor's mom appeared out on the back terrace, saw him, and waved with a huge smile on her face.

"Hi, angel!" The thick trees and carefully cut hedges absorbed the sound of her voice, making it seem small, but the affection was unmistakable.

Sam waved back and felt like a rat.

52

SAM

"I'm sorry," Sam said into the phone. "I shouldn't have said that. It was stupid."

Trevor remained silent.

Sam tried not to choke on his words. He spoke softly. "I grew up without a mom, is all. I just thought, you know, she's out there somewhere. She's my mom, even if you don't want her to be yours, and everything for you is so easy. I snap my fingers around this place and people are running to get me Skittles or sushi or make the movie my dad's been dreaming about for twelve years. So all of a sudden it seems like I can have *anything* I want, and I want her."

Trevor finally took a deep breath on the other end. "I get it."

Sam said, "And you accept my apology? I really mean it. I feel stupid. Your mom's not bad. She's waving at me right now and grinning like a jack-o'-lantern."

Trevor laughed like he'd seen that before and seemed to change gears. "It's okay. And don't worry, Wolf won't hurt you. Dolph has him trained like nothing you've ever seen."

"He knows I'm not you, though, I tell you that."

"He's smart, that's all," Trevor said. "Man, this is like eating spaghetti with a spoon. I mean, we're kids. How complicated can our lives be?"

"Like spiderwebs."

"You're telling me. That Klum? What a jerk."

"I know."

"Listen, will you do me a favor?" Trevor asked.

"Of course."

"If you can find her—your mom—go ahead. But promise me you won't tell her about me, and you have to promise that you won't contact her until you're you again, and I'm me."

"But once she sees me," Sam said, "she'll know about you. I look just like you now."

"She won't bother me if you tell her not to."

"Why do you think that?"

"Because you'll tell her what I said."

"What did you say?"

"That when she gave me away, she turned her back on me, and no one turns their back on me and gets away with it. Tell her I don't want to see her. Ever. You tell her that. She'll stay away."

It was Sam's turn to go quiet.

"You there?" Trevor asked.

"Yeah, I'm here. Thanks. I better go. Your mom looks like she really wants to see me—you."

189

"Yeah, you better. She doesn't like to wait. Thanks for the advice on the curveball. I can't believe it's as easy as that dot."

"Some people can't see the dot."

"I guess I'm a natural baseball player."

Sam laughed. "And I might be a natural actor. I'm not bad."

"Okay, good luck."

"And good luck to you in the game. Just get along with Klum. The real way to get him back is to get into USC Elite. When that happens, he'll get everything he deserves, and trust me. I *will* beat him."

53

TREVOR

A fat orange sun crawled up over the lip of the dark blue hills. The last of the birds ended their morning songs and settled in for the coming heat. As Trevor scuffed his feet along the driveway outside the trailer, the smell of the landfill crept through the cool shadows and up his nose. He sniffed and turned away from the sunrise. He thought of his own yard, the smell of cut grass and flowers and the towering trees that shaded them from the sun. Beside the trailer sat a stack of used tires, a broken toilet, and a rusted refrigerator, junk that might have come to life and crept up out of the landfill so that what Trevor saw was almost as nasty as what he smelled.

Trevor shook his head and set out on a mission to retrieve Sam's bat bag from the tiny bedroom. The trailer door opened with a creak, and inside Sam's father emerged from the shower drying his hair. "Already dressed and ready to go?"

Trevor shrugged. "Couldn't sleep."

"Nervous?" Sam's dad wrinkled his brow. "You never get nervous."

Trevor turned away. "I want to get there early and work this curveball some more, get my groove back, that's all."

When Trevor emerged from Sam's bedroom with the bat bag, Sam's dad had two bowls of cereal out on the table and orange juice in paper cups.

"I'm good."

"You'll be good with breakfast in you."

"Why do they say that, anyway? Do you really believe it?"

Sam's dad looked up. "You feeling okay?"

"Sure," Trevor said. He sat down and spooned in a few mouthfuls of cereal, chewing mechanically and forcing himself to swallow.

He set his spoon down and looked at his watch.

"Okay, I get it." Sam's dad picked up the bowl and tilted it toward his face, finishing it before he got up, took Trevor's bowl, and put them both in the sink. "Let's go."

Trevor followed him out. They rode to the practice field without talking. When they pulled into the parking lot, Sam's dad said, "Don't forget, after batting practice you're going to ride to the game with Coach Sharp. I'll meet you there."

Trevor remembered to kiss and hug Sam's dad before jogging off to batting practice. Sam was the first player there, and Coach Sharp seemed happy to pump some curveballs through the pitching machine in the small cage beside the field. Trevor screwed up his face and focused on the pitches, getting into a good groove by the time the other Blue Sox players and assistant coaches showed up.

Coach Sharp checked his watch and called them all together, reminding them that they'd practice batting for an hour before they got into his and his assistants' cars and rode to the game field as a team. Trevor had a thin sweat going by the time they finished. The excitement continued to build, and by the time Trevor climbed into the backseat of Coach Sharp's Tahoe, he couldn't hold still.

"Quit shaking your leg, will you?" Cole Price said, turning around in the front seat. "Your knee is in my back."

"Sorry." Trevor grabbed his knee with both hands to stop it.

Coach Sharp played a soul CD from the eighties, stuff Trevor and the rest of the kids never heard of but that Coach Sharp sang along to as if they weren't there. When they pulled off the highway and passed Dodger Stadium, Trevor's nervousness only increased. The memory of his embarrassing experience with the Dodgers a few days ago churned his stomach as they rode to a far corner of Elysian Park. The stands were already filled with spectators. Parents and friends of the Blue Sox players wore blue and red, but plenty of people were there in the purple and white of Palos Verdes, whose team warmed up on the grass.

"Here we go, boys," Coach Sharp said, putting his truck into park.

They piled out and unloaded their gear in the dugout. Trevor sat there with Frankie and RJ, waiting for Palos Verdes to get off the field. His stomach flopped around in his belly like a walrus. The excitement he had imagined he would feel choked under the grip of jangling nerves.

"They look big," Frankie said.

"They stink," RJ said. "They lost ten-to-two to that San Diego Sharks team we beat in the Pasadena tournament by five."

"Never judge a team by its past performance. On any given day, any team can beat another," Frankie said. "That's what Dad says, 'on any given day.'"

"Dad was a lacrosse player." RJ left the bench as if that were the final and decisive point of the argument.

Trevor warmed up with the team, unable to shake his nerves. During the national anthem, he had to cross his legs, then quickly find a bathroom when it was over. He was horrified upon his return to see that the first two batters had already struck out and he was up.

"Sam, you okay?" Coach Sharp put his hands on Trevor's shoulders.

Trevor could only nod as he scooped up a helmet and Sam's bat from the rack where he'd left it. "Fine."

"Okay, well, go get him. Watch out for the changeup. He's throwing heat, but we know he's got that pitch."

Trevor took slow steps toward the plate. The sun, well above the trees, shone bright and hot. Dust swirled on a small breeze along with the smell of hot dogs and cut grass. It was a setting worthy of a sports movie, but none of it held any of the thrill Trevor had imagined it would.

Instead, he had to choke back the acid creeping up into his throat. Instead of the pitcher, all Trevor could think about was how glad he was that if he did lose it, his breakfast wouldn't make too big of a mess because he barely ate.

Gone was the joy of competing and the excitement of the game. Everything was vomit and nerves and trembling muscles.

Trevor swung his bat a few times but felt almost nothing below his elbows, not his hands, not the grip, not the bat. The umpire cleared his throat and told Trevor to get going. Trevor stepped into the box. The pitcher wound up and threw a burner, right down the pipe.

Trevor shut his eyes and swung.

54

SAM

Sam woke up late. He lay still, remembering where was and who he was supposed to be, then stretched and yawned, enjoying it. Trevor's phone blinked a red eye at him from the bedside table, letting Sam know there were messages waiting. He ignored them because he could and stepped into the shower. He whistled to himself as he scrubbed his body and hair, then dried off with a puffy warm towel.

Trees cooled the air, and the hint of a breeze brought the scent of orange trees with it through the open windows. Sam stepped out onto the terrace and looked along the north side of the mansion and out over the lawn, marveling that one family could live in a place big enough for at least a hundred people.

The chop of a helicopter as it cruised over the treetops above dropped a weight in his gut. He was excited because he'd never ridden in a helicopter, and happy it would fly him over the heavy beach traffic to the home in Malibu. But it would also bring him that much closer to his meeting with Trevor's father—due in on their private jet from Australia. That was the good news Trevor's mom had given him yesterday in the garden, and Sam did his best to act excited.

Downstairs, Sam appeared in the breakfast room wearing a Joe Girardi Cubs jersey over a pair of Michael Jordan shorts. Trevor's mom sat not in her robe and turban, but dressed in shorts and a snug jacket that looked like something a band leader would wear. Her hair fell like billowing fog around her face, blond and shiny, and her face had been carefully made up with scarlet lipstick to match her jacket. She was texting as she talked on the phone, and she sipped coffee as she picked over a croissant filled with jam.

The smell of fresh bacon and scrambled eggs cut through the scent of fresh-cut flowers in vases around the room. The thought of food overcame Sam's distress over meeting Trevor's dad. He loaded his plate and sat down across from Trevor's mom. She gave him a quick wave and blew him a kiss, pointing to her phone. Sam nodded that he understood and dug in.

Sunshine, flowers, and rich green bushes and trees glittering with dewdrops filled the big bay window. Below the flowery terraces dancing with little yellow birds, a waterfall gurgled into the pool. Sam couldn't help comparing the sights and smells to his own cramped trailer and landfill. The tinkle of crystal glasses and silver utensils against thin china plates were a world away from the sawing of plastic knives, the tearing of paper plates, and the hollow thump of wax-covered cups set down on a plastic tabletop. Sam ate until he was ready to burst, and Trevor's mom finally got off the phone.

"You ready, angel?"

Sam looked down at himself, wondering if he was dressed right or if there was something he needed to bring. "Sure."

"Good, come on."

Sam followed Trevor's mom. They walked back into the house to the elevator and stepped into its spacious wood-paneled car.

"Oh, your father has to leave first thing in the morning, so I don't know if you want to invite a friend for tomorrow, but you can. I've got a party you wouldn't want to go to in the afternoon."

Sam felt his heart leap. "Can I invite McKenna?"

Trevor's mom put on a big pair of sunglasses and pushed the elevator button before she smiled at him. "McKenna? Of course. She'll have to have someone drive her out. We can't keep your father waiting."

Up they went, emerging out onto the roof beneath a small pavilion. Across a short stretch of the flat roof, a silver helicopter waited with its blades still. Thomas stood beside it at the top of a set of steps. As they approached, he opened the door. Sam followed Trevor's mom, stepping inside a cabin dressed out in glimmering red-brown wood, leather, and brass. They sat next to each other in comfortable bucket seats. Thomas stepped in and closed the door, speaking in a low voice to the pilots before he sat stiffly in one of the remaining four empty seats.

The engines whirred, and the blade began to chop. Trevor's mom took out her phone and smiled at him. "Got to tweet a bit.

Stu was bugging me about that. I'm sure you do yours without thinking."

Sam nodded and realized that he had neglected Trevor's tweet. He took out Trevor's phone and got onto his page. He felt a thrill scamper up his spine as the helicopter lifted off the roof. The earth below him sank away. The huge mansion, pool, and gardens quickly became a small design, then they surged forward, passing over the hilltops and mansions of the other wildly wealthy people of Bel Air.

Sam quickly typed into the phone:

> riding the helicopter to Malibu. Dad is bk from Australia 4 a day at the beach.
> Life is good ;)

Sam read it over and giggled to himself before sending it. Who would believe?

Below, the snarling traffic of LA jammed the highways as the rest of the world tried desperately to get to the waiting ocean and waves. Thomas sat staring straight ahead, the picture of a storefront mannequin. Sam looked at his phone for the time. He knew that right about now, Trevor and his team must be taking the field against Palos Verdes. They could win without Sam, that he knew. He wondered if Trevor would think the deal was worth it. It was hard to imagine how that could be: preferring a Saturday morning ball game to riding in your personal helicopter to Malibu? Sam shook his head.

The ocean glinted with sunshine. Ragged lines of waves drifted toward a beach already dotted with umbrellas and chairs for the day in front of the homes stacked up on the dunes. They descended to one of the biggest places Sam could see, landing on the roof and getting off as the blades still whirled above them, entering a pavilion and elevator that seemed like a brother to the one in the Bel Air mansion. Sam couldn't believe it, but to Trevor's mom it was clearly no big deal.

Down they went into the house. Sam was distracted by the marble sculptures, modern paintings, and odd-shaped windows looking out over the glittering ocean. He tried not to gawk, but he knew his eyes were wide and he just couldn't keep his jaw from dropping. Before he knew it, they were walking out onto a half-round terrace facing the waves. The surf crashed. Sam smelled the sand and the ocean. Leaning out over the balcony was a man in swim trunks and a short-sleeve beach shirt. The breeze lifted his silver hair. His skin was tan and muscular.

Trevor's mom said, "Darling!"

The man turned around. He was smaller than Sam expected, and his face instead of scowling and serious—like he was in all the pictures Sam had seen—was smiling and relaxed.

"Diana." He kissed Trevor's mom long enough to make Sam look down at his feet. "Trevor. Come here, Son."

Sam looked up and crossed the terrace, shaking the Hollywood giant's outstretched hand.

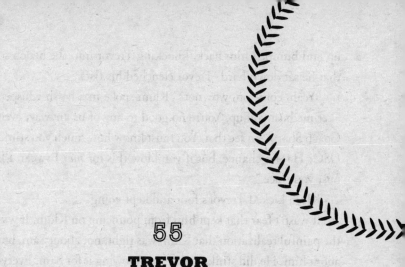

55

TREVOR

Trevor struck out, three times. He committed two errors in the field—plays he *knew* he could make but choked on. Coach Sharp couldn't even look at him anymore. Sweat soaked Trevor's uniform, and a layer of dust caked his skin from a dive he took into the dirt to snag a grounder. His knee hurt, and the underside of his forearm was scraped and bleeding.

Trevor sat in the dugout and sighed. He couldn't wait to get back home, where things were nice and easy and no one dared to scowl at him. The whole thing was awful, and he asked himself what he'd been thinking. The Blue Sox were losing, too. With just one inning to go, they were down by a run. Their last batter of the inning struck out, and the Palos Verdes crowd cheered. Trevor reached under the bench for Sam's glove, got hold of it, and stood to take the field.

When he did, he bumped into Dorian Klum. Klum tensed

up and bumped him back, knocking Trevor into the bench so that he sat down hard. Trevor clenched his fists.

"Yeah, come on, why not?" Klum spoke in a harsh whisper. "Let me bust you up. You're no good to any of us anyway; even Coach Sharp can see that. You must know how much you stink. USC? Ha, fat chance, but if you blow this for *me*? I swear, I'll bust your face."

Klum kicked Trevor's foot and kept going.

It wasn't fear that kept him from pouncing on Klum. It was the painful realization that Klum was right, not about Sam, but about him. He did stink, and he was blowing it for Sam. Everyone expected the Blue Sox to destroy the Palos Verdes team. This was just the quarterfinals of the big tournament. Palos Verdes was the last seed of the entire tournament. Trevor knew from his teammates' talk that the two wins Palos Verdes got just to get to the quarterfinals were the result of some incredible luck. This time—if Palos Verdes won—it would be because of some very poor play by the Blue Sox, especially Trevor's.

And, if the Blue Sox did lose? Sam (and Klum) wouldn't get the chance to be the tournament's MVP, because they wouldn't even make it to the championship. Although he didn't know Sam well, Trevor felt pretty certain that if that happened, Sam might do something crazy. Who knew, he might tell the whole story to everyone, embarrassing Trevor's parents and putting Trevor's relationship with them under a permanent cloud. Even if Sam didn't do something foolish, Trevor knew the USC dream was the one thing Sam had, and Trevor didn't want to cost him that one thing.

He stood back up and jogged out onto the field, settling

into his position between second and third base and throwing the ball around the horn to warm up with the rest of the infield. Klum stood on the mound, a big beast with a snarling face. The inning went quickly, and Sam didn't get any action at shortstop. Klum sent two down swinging, and a third popped out to center field. The Blue Sox jogged back to the dugout.

Coach Sharp called them together into a knot.

"I told you guys. I warned you, didn't I?" The coach made a point to look at Trevor. "But obviously, some of you didn't listen when I said this team was good enough to beat us and send us home. No championship, nobody on our team being MVP, and no USC Elite Training Center. Well, here we are. It's the last inning, and we're almost at the top of the order. We're one run down. *One.* You know and I know we can get that back, so let's do it. We've worked too hard and come too far to lose to this team. Come on, bring it in."

The players grasped Coach Sharp's fist.

"Focus on three," the coach growled. "One, two, three . . ."

"FOCUS!"

The last two batters in the order promptly struck out, leaving Frankie up at the top of the order with RJ on deck and Trevor on double deck.

Trevor hated to admit it, but if Frankie or RJ struck out and ended it, he wouldn't mind. His confidence was shot, and he didn't want the pressure of having to get a hit when the game was on the line. He shook his head in a fit of anger, asking himself how he could think like that.

Frankie stepped into the batter's box and swung at the first two pitches, missing both.

"Come *on*, Frankie. You can do it!" RJ's face turned red.

The pitcher wound up and threw. Frankie swung and connected. The ball took off down the third-base line. Frankie sprinted for first. The third baseman scooped up the ball and made the throw, beating Frankie to the bag.

"Safe!" The umpire chopped his hands sideways, and Trevor saw that the first baseman had taken his foot off the bag stretching to make the catch.

Everyone cheered and RJ marched to the plate, swinging his bat. Trevor stepped into the warm-up circle and put a weighted donut on his bat to make it feel lighter when he removed it if he got to the plate himself.

RJ let the first pitch go, a ball. He swung on the second and sent it foul. The Blue Sox cheered.

"You got it, RJ!" Trevor shouted, caught up in the excitement.

RJ swung at the next pitch and missed. Miraculously, he let the next three pitches go, all balls, and RJ walked to first, advancing Frankie to second.

"Sam! Sam! Sam!" the team cheered.

Coach Sharp stopped Trevor, resting hands on his shoulders. "Relax. That's the beauty of this game. Forget the fact that you've been out of sync. You can get it right back. We both know what you've done today isn't the real Sam Palomaki."

Trevor gasped and searched the coach's eyes for something more accusing than a pep talk, but that's all it was.

"You're as good as the next pitch, Sam. Go get him."

Trevor felt jittery as he stepped up to the plate. He let the first pitch go, a ball. He felt frozen, hoping the pitcher was tired and would do him the same favor he'd done RJ by walking him on base. That wasn't happening. Trevor let the next two balls pass, both strikes, without a thought of swinging. With a 1–2 count, he had to try. The game—and maybe Sam Palomaki's future—was on the line.

He shook his head and slapped his own face, jarring himself out of the daze the way he did when he needed to do a fresh take on a movie set. Feeling better, he blinked and looked up into the stands, where he saw Sam's dad urging him on. By the look on the father's face, Trevor knew it was more than just Sam's dream on the line.

He hunkered down and focused. The pitcher wound up and his arm whipped forward, firing the pitch. In the instant that it flew at him, Trevor saw the red dot and knew what it meant.

He clenched his jaw and reared back.

Then he swung.

56
SAM

Trevor's dad pulled Sam into a warm hug, and then he pulled Trevor's mom in as well so that the three of them stood there. Trevor's dad put his face against the stubble on Sam's head and laughed, hugging him tighter still before letting go.

"It's so good to see you both," he said.

"Then you should stay more than a day," Trevor's mom said, sulking a bit.

Trevor's dad chucked her lightly under the chin. "I'll make up for it. When this is over, we'll spend two weeks in Paris. I booked the presidential suite at the Ritz."

This made Trevor's mom smile and kiss the father again. When she finally let go, he said, "Love, can I have Trevor for a few minutes before lunch?"

"Really? Why?"

Trevor's dad laughed in a lighthearted way. "One of

those father and son things."

"Ahhh." She kissed the father again, then Sam on the head before turning back toward the house. "I want to take a swim in the ocean anyway. Ta-ta, boys."

Sam watched her go, afraid to be alone with Trevor's dad, even though he seemed nice so far.

"Come on, Son." Trevor's dad put an arm around Sam's shoulder. "Let's take a walk."

On the elevator ride down to the beach, Trevor's dad asked about *Dragon's Empire*, how it was going, and whether or not Pierce Everette had had one of his famous temper tantrums yet. Sam gave one-word answers, too nervous about the need to take a walk on the beach to discuss something, and wondering if it was what brought Trevor's dad home. Sam hadn't planned to even see Trevor's dad. Trevor had assured him that the Hollywood mogul would be in Australia the entire time they were pinch-hitting for each other.

They walked away from the house and toward the rough coastline to the west where the beach ended. Salty spray rode the breeze, and above gulls shrieked and wheeled in the air. Trevor's dad kept glancing back, and Sam saw him nod when Trevor's mom jogged down the sand and into the water. They passed three more houses before Trevor's dad turned up toward the dunes. Sam followed him away from the ocean, between the houses, and out onto the sandy road. They doubled back to the Goldman mansion, entering the front door in the face of a silent butler. Sam was too afraid to ask what in the world they were doing.

Trevor's dad led him into the house and a wood-paneled

library. Leather books packed shelves that stretched sixteen feet to the carved ceiling. The father sat down behind a desk in a thick leather chair.

"Have a seat, Son." Trevor's dad pointed to a stuffed leather chair in front of the desk.

Sam sat and tucked his hands under his legs to keep them from flapping like the gulls he'd seen outside.

"We need to talk."

Trevor's dad stared at Sam with moist eyes. Sam thought Trevor's dad might even cry. Sam had no idea what he was about to say.

"Okay," Sam said.

Trevor's dad picked up the phone on his desk, waited a moment, then said, "Yes, show them in."

The door behind Sam opened, and Sam couldn't believe what he saw.

57

SAM

Sara Grant burst into the room wearing a business suit with her chin held high. Beside her was a hulking man with a bald head and handlebar mustache Sam recognized from TV. Dale Moffit wore a black T-shirt and jeans, and his muscular arms crawled with tattoos. His pale blue eyes glittered at Sam.

Sam felt sick. Before Trevor's father said a word, he knew that Sara Grant had snitched on him. The private detective was her proof of his unauthorized search for his biological parents.

"You know these people, Trevor?" Trevor's dad asked.

Sam met Sara's eyes. She wore the smug look of a queen handing out punishment.

Sam nodded. "Yes."

"I told you he wouldn't try to deny it," Trevor's father said.

Sam glanced at the father and saw that he was speaking to

Sara Grant. Sara's expression changed. Her mouth opened but no words came out.

Finally, her eyes flashed at Sam and she said, "Caught in the act, I guess."

Trevor's dad cleared his throat. "Or just honest."

"You know, Mr. Goldman," Sara Grant said, sounding out of breath, "that whatever I can do to help you, I'm happy to do."

"I appreciate that."

"And I just knew this was something you'd want to be aware of."

"Yes." Trevor's father clasped his hands and placed them under his chin. "You're right about that. Trevor is too young to make these kinds of decisions, and, given his situation, I know there are a lot of people who'd do favors for him when maybe they shouldn't.

"Thank you also for bringing Mr. Moffit."

Trevor's dad nodded at the man with the big mustache. Moffit's smile revealed a single gold tooth.

"Ms. Grant," Trevor's dad said, "please call my office Monday. Ask for Vera and tell her I want you to have the Lightstar account."

"The animation studio?" Sara Grant's eyes widened with greed. Sam knew by the size of her smile that the deal was going to put a ton of money in Sara's pockets.

"Yes, I'd say that's fair. Of course you know I expect complete confidentiality about all this."

Sara grinned like a well-fed cat. "That goes without saying."

"Thank you," Trevor's dad said. "Now, unless there's anything else, I'd like to have a private word with Mr. Moffit."

The tone in Trevor's dad's voice meant there better not be anything else. Sara Grant must have known that because she left in a blink, without even a glance at Sam.

"Mr. Moffit, please, sit down." Trevor's dad pointed to a chair beside Sam, and the muscular man took it. "I take it you haven't begun the search Trevor wanted to send you on."

Moffit shook his head ever so slightly. "Sara has her ways, and I've learned it's best to follow her lead."

"But you *could* find my son's biological parents?"

Sam stared at Trevor's father. The man's face hardened, and his jaw jutted out at Moffit in a challenging way .

Moffit seemed to chose his words carefully. "If . . . they can be found, I can find them."

"And that means?" Trevor's father asked.

"Sometimes people can't be found. Sometimes they don't want to be found."

"Is that more likely than not in your experience?"

"In my experience, I usually find what I'm looking for, Mr. Goldman. There have been times when that's not happened. Rare times."

"Good," Trevor's father said. "If my son wants to find his biological mother, I want you to do that for him. I'm going back to Australia in the morning. I don't want emails or text messages or any communication except in person. Until I get back, you'll communicate directly with Trevor. I'll see that you have access to him at the studio. I will pay you twice your normal rate and insist on complete confidentiality, including from Ms. Grant. She's the second-to-last person I'd want to know."

"Second?" Moffit raised an eyebrow.

"The one person who must never know about this . . . is my wife."

58

TREVOR

The crack of the bat on that ball was a sound and a feeling Trevor knew he'd never forget. The ball took off. Trevor ran, and as he did he seemed to float, and everything slowed down for him.

The center fielder and the right fielder both scrambled to get under the ball, but it was deep in the field and Trevor thought it might even clear the fence. Frankie rounded third. Trevor's foot slapped first and the base coach signaled him to stay. From the corner of his eye, he saw the two outfielders bump each other and stumble before one of them came up with the ball, hop-skipped, and fired it back toward the infield. The second baseman got into position for the cutoff. Frankie scored and RJ rounded third.

As Trevor bounced up and down, the second baseman made the throw to home. RJ lowered his head, arms and legs pumping. The ball smacked the catcher's mitt. RJ slid, kicking up a cloud of dust. All that mattered was the umpire's call at home plate.

Trevor clenched his hands and teeth.

59

TREVOR

The umpire reared up like a circus elephant. "Safe!"

The Blue Sox fans went wild. The team rushed from the dugout, hugging RJ and Frankie. When Trevor reached the mob at home plate, they lifted him on their shoulders. Everyone slapped him high fives—everyone except Dorian Klum and his buddy, Scotty Needum. The rest of the team finally put Trevor down, and several of them hugged him tight before they lined up to shake hands with the downtrodden team from Palos Verdes.

Even shaking the other team's hands was a thrill for Trevor, and he felt genuine sadness for their downcast faces and the occasional tear, because he knew what they were feeling. It was how he'd felt only a few minutes ago, only when he felt it, it wasn't as final as what they were feeling. They were done, out of the tournament, and he suspected that some of their players, especially the pitcher, had dreams like Sam's, of making the USC Elite Training Center.

Trevor forgot about the losers, though, as he gathered around Coach Sharp outside their dugout with the rest of the Blue Sox.

"Guys," the coach said, his voice rough and worn down from yelling, "that was an ugly win, but a great one. They're all great, aren't they?"

Everyone cheered, until Coach Sharp held up his hand.

"But the lesson I want you all to remember was what happened to Sam today."

All eyes turned toward Trevor, and his face burned with delight and embarrassment at the same time. Not even the evil looks Klum and Needum gave him could spoil the moment.

"And I want you guys to take that lesson with you, not just through your baseball careers, but through your lives, because there are gonna be times in your life like Sam had today. Times when nothing is going right. Times when you're not yourself, or maybe you're just unlucky. But you keep going, like he did."

Coach Sharp nodded at Trevor. "You *keep going* and *that's* what gives you a chance to *win*. And when you win like that, when you pull it out of a disastrous start, well, Sam, you tell them. Isn't it about as sweet as anything you can ever imagine?"

Trevor beamed back at them all, not Sam's teammates anymore, not Sam's coaches, but *his*. Whether they knew who he really was or not, the Blue Sox were *his* team, and this moment belonged to Trevor Goldman. Trevor could barely swallow, his throat was so choked up with emotion. But he nodded and grinned like a maniac until his teammates burst out laughing and patted him on the back.

Trevor could have stayed there all night, but he had to accept that it was time to go. He packed up Sam's bat bag, then accepted a hug and a kiss from Sam's dad.

"You were great," Sam's dad said.

"Not until that last hit."

"When we needed it most."

Trevor sighed with pleasure. As they pulled away from the park, he could only think about one thing. This couldn't be his last game. He *had* to keep going. Feeling like a pathetic loser through most of the game only made his two winning RBIs that much sweeter. It only made the whole day that much more unforgettable. The feeling of playing, and competing, and *winning*—it was like nothing else he'd ever experienced, and at that moment, for the first time in his life, he wished with all his heart that he wasn't Trevor Goldman. He wished he were Sam Palomaki.

Trevor also knew that to be awash in the thrill of another win, he would do just about anything.

60

SAM

Sam couldn't believe his ears.

Trevor's dad scowled at Moffit, the private investigator. "Is that understood?"

"If I couldn't keep my mouth shut, I wouldn't be the best PI in Los Angeles, and I am the best PI in Los Angeles."

"Call my office Monday. Ask for Nora. Send me an agreement, but you can begin now. My word is all you need."

"I know that, Mr. Goldman."

"Do you need anything from me?" Trevor's dad asked. "Birth certificate? Adoption papers?"

Moffit smiled. "I already have all that, Mr. Goldman."

Trevor's dad raised his eyebrows.

"I told you, I'm the best."

"But you haven't begun the search?" Trevor's dad said.

"No, just the background information I need. The internet

is a beautiful thing." Trevor's dad stood and shook hands with Moffit before the PI left the room. Trevor's dad circled the desk and sat down next to Sam. "Are you okay?"

Sam blinked at him. "Sure."

"Surprised?"

Sam nodded. He was surprised. Surprised and confused.

Trevor's dad seemed to read his face. "Your mother wouldn't understand, but I do. You see, Trevor, I was adopted myself. I know how it feels, and I told myself when we got you that if you ever wanted to find your biological mother . . . and even your biological father, I'd help. Honestly, I expected this."

The room seemed to be spinning and tilting at the same time. Sam felt so many things: sadness, fear, confusion, even anger. Mixed into all these feelings was the fact that Sam knew he wasn't even the person Trevor's dad thought he was. It was hard to focus. It was like a crazy dream.

Trevor's dad put a hand on Sam's shoulder. "I just thought it would be later in your life, not now. You're young and you have . . . well, you have everything, don't you?"

Sam nodded and knew that it was true. Trevor Goldman had *everything*, and part of Sam felt bad because he knew it wasn't Trevor who wanted to find their mother; it was him. Maybe it was because Sam didn't have everything. Maybe that was why, and Sam had to ask himself if it was fair. What was Trevor getting out of the deal? He got to play in a couple baseball games. Big deal. Sam's payoff was to get a green light for his father's script, to make a dream come true for the most important person in his life. That was the deal. Wasn't *that* enough?

Sam felt horrible, because he knew it should have been enough.

219

His eyes filled with tears, and he wasn't even quite sure why.

"Do you want to talk about all this?" Trevor's dad asked.

Sam shook his head.

"I understand. Come on, let's get back out on the beach. Your mother will wonder where we went."

Sam followed Trevor's dad back the way they'd come. As they walked up the beach, Sam saw that someone had set up several chairs and umbrellas in the sand behind the Goldman mansion. Trevor's mom lay back in the sun, wearing her big dark glasses and reading a magazine.

She looked up and smiled as they approached. "Where'd you go, Santa Clara?"

"Almost." Trevor's father bent down and kissed her again before plopping down in a chair beside her.

Sam hesitated, then sat down, too. He took off his shirt, and the sun warmed his skin. Trevor's dad offered him a soda from the cooler before opening a sparkling water for himself.

Trevor's father put one hand on his wife's leg and the other on Sam's shoulder and sighed. "How lucky are we, Diana? How lucky? Trevor?"

Sam thought about the promise he'd made to Trevor, the promise not to try to contact their mother until he was Sam Palomaki again. Everything was different now. Trevor's dad was involved. *He* was the one who sent Moffit off to find her. Sam had no idea what he should do. Only one thing was for sure.

The promise he made to Trevor had been broken.

61

TREVOR

The Blue Sox all met at Pizza Hut. The players spit wads of straw wrappings at one another and hooted with delight as they slugged down pitchers of soda and stuffed-crust pizza. The parents chattered and laughed themselves at their own table in the corner. Trevor had never seen anything like it. When his parents mingled with other people, there was always a rigid formality, as if they were a king and queen who had a court of followers glad for even the smallest word of recognition. He'd never seen parents having almost as good a time as the kids themselves.

Trevor sat on the end of the table surrounded by Cole, Frankie, and RJ. It was easy for Trevor to understand why they were Sam's best friends.

"Okay, what do you think of this?" Frankie raised a leg and let one rip.

They all held their noses and laughed.

Cole turned to Frankie and, still pinching his nose, said, "I think your voice is changing, but your breath still smells the same."

When RJ heard that, the soda he was sipping through a straw exploded out his nose, spraying Frankie's pizza. Trevor laughed so hard at the whole thing that tears streamed down his face, and he had to excuse himself to use the bathroom. He was still laughing when he walked in and found himself face-to-face with Dorian Klum.

Klum jabbed a finger in Trevor's chest and pushed his face forward until their noses nearly met. "What's so funny, tough guy?"

Trevor slapped Klum's finger away and slipped past him.

"You better run."

"I'm not running." Trevor turned around, his hands turning into fists, even though he knew he had to keep his cool.

"Maybe you're laughing at the way you played today. That was some joke. You actually think you're in competition with me for MVP? You think USC wants some chump that goes one for five in a *Junior League* game? Heck, what was I today? Four for five with two home runs? Oh yeah, they'll really be thinking about you. Ha!"

Klum turned and flung open the door, banging it against the wall and laughing to himself as he returned to the tables. Trevor did what he'd come for, then washed his hands. In the mirror, he studied his face. The joy of the win was suddenly fading fast.

He shook his head, refusing to let Klum ruin the day.

"You made that hit and won the game," he said to himself

in the mirror. "*You* did that, no one else. Klum. He's like a fart. He stinks bad, but just hold your breath, and before you know it, he's gone."

Trevor smiled and decided his buddies would like that, so he returned to the table and told them. They all laughed and stole secret looks at Klum, who sat leaned back in his chair at the other table with two straws sticking out of his nose.

Someone shouted out the idea to go to the Schmellings to swim in their pool. Frankie and RJ's mom stood up and said it was a good idea and everyone cheered. The players went home for bathing suits, and they all spent the rest of the day swimming and splashing around, playing sharks and minnows as well as Marco Polo. By the time Trevor got back to the trailer, he was exhausted. Sam's dad took some frozen dinners out of the freezer and stuck them in the microwave. While he was waiting, Trevor felt Sam's phone buzz. He went into Sam's bedroom and checked the text. Sam wanted to talk to him, and he wanted to talk to Sam.

"I'm gonna get some air," Trevor said to Sam's dad.

"Are you talking to that McKenna girl?" Sam's dad asked.

Trevor faked embarrassment by looking away. He shrugged without making a commitment either way and hustled out the front door. Once he was beyond earshot of the trailer, Trevor dialed up his own cell phone.

Sam answered.

62

SAM

Sam sat on the balcony overlooking the ocean. The sun melted into a pool of red, and the ocean hissed against the sand. In one hand he held a grape soda, in the other was a half-eaten Twinkie. Sam's dad wasn't much for junk food, and Twinkies he called chemical bombs. Sam loved them, and grape soda, too. So when Thomas, the butler, asked him if there was anything he'd like, Sam decided to go for it.

He needed a distraction while he waited for Trevor to call him, and even though there was a perfectly good Xbox in Trevor's bedroom and a couple of unread books, Sam found himself drawn to the ocean. Its clean breeze and sleepy sounds beneath a haze of late-day sunshine seemed to blunt the razor edge of his nerves. It was hard for Sam to believe that such a place was only miles from a big, dirty city like LA.

The phone rang. Trevor. Sam took a deep breath and answered it.

"How you doing?" Sam asked.

"We need to talk."

"I know. I'm the one who texted you." Sam lowered his voice and looked around beneath the balcony to make sure no one could hear. "You're not going to be happy."

"Why? What happened?"

"Your dad found out about me looking for our mom, our biological mom. I didn't tell him, I swear. It was that Sara Grant. McKenna asked her for a private detective and said she could keep a secret. She went right to your dad to kiss up to him."

"He knows about *us*?"

"No, no," Sam said. "He still thinks I'm you."

"Did my mother go bananas?" Trevor asked.

"She doesn't know, and your father doesn't want her to know."

"What did he say? Is he mad?"

Sam stood up and paced the small balcony. "No. He said he understood. Trevor, your dad was adopted. He said he expected it. He wants to help, but we—you, me—have to keep it quiet."

Trevor groaned.

"I think it'll all be fine," Sam said. "Really. Trevor? You okay?"

Sam could hear Trevor breathing, but it was nearly a minute before he spoke. "You owe me for this, Sam. We agreed finding our mother was *not* part of the deal, so you owe me big."

"Okay," Sam said, "I know I owe you."

"So *this* is what I want," Trevor said. "I want to play two more games, your league game on Tuesday and the tournament semifinals on Saturday. I think McKenna's having a pool party on Sunday. We can make the switch there."

"The semifinals?" Sam said. "They might need me for that."

"I won the game today."

"*You* won the game?"

"I hit a two-run single in the bottom of the sixth. We were one run down. Sam, you should have seen it."

"How were you one run down against Palos Verdes?" Sam knew the team from the south wasn't that good. Everyone had been talking about how lucky they'd been just to get to the quarterfinals.

"I had to get my groove."

"You choked?"

"I didn't choke; I had to find my rhythm."

Sam nodded, thinking. "Listen, I mean it. I feel terrible about this thing with your dad."

"Right, and this is how you can make it up to me, Sam. I want to *play*. I'm good. One more week, two more games. That should be enough time for the investigator to find your mom—our mom, I guess. Don't expect me to follow through with it if we switch back."

"You said I could find her as long as you didn't know."

"I said I'd get your dad's script a green light. That's what *I* said. This whole thing with finding our biological parents was your invention. No way is that part of the deal, and you know it. You're playing with fire."

"Your dad said he expected it." Sam heard the pleading in his own voice.

He looked down below. At the far corner of the house,

Trevor's parents emerged and sat down on the terrace, each with a big glass of red wine. Trevor's dad wore the same friendly smile Sam had been so surprised at first to see. "I bet he'd be okay with all this."

"What does that mean?" Trevor's voice dropped.

Sam shrugged to himself. "I bet if we came clean with your dad—told him the whole thing about how we're pinch-hitting for each other—that he'd be okay, that he'd help me find our mom, keep you out of it, let you play Saturday, *and* help my dad get his green light."

Trevor stayed silent for a moment before he let out a short, tattered burst of laughter. "Are you crazy?"

"What? He's a great guy. Maybe you don't appreciate it because he's your dad, but trust me. You should have seen his face when he told me *he* was adopted. He's a sweet guy, your dad."

"Trust me, no one has mistaken my dad for a sweet guy since he stopped wearing diapers, and even then I highly doubt it."

"Trevor, I feel the same way about my dad."

"*Your* dad is a teacher. He quotes Shakespeare and helps kids learn to read. Do *not*, I repeat, *do not* mistake my dad for anything close to that. I love him. He's generous with me and my mom, but that's about it. Don't even think about telling him what we're doing. I'm not so much worried about me, but you? Don't do it. Just don't."

"Whatever," Sam said.

"It's not 'whatever.'"

"Okay, I heard you."

"So, I can pinch-hit for you? One more week? Please?"

63

SAM

"You know what's at stake here, right?" Sam scowled so hard he thought Trevor might sense it over the phone.

"You mean that we have to win in the semifinals, right?"

"That's right," Sam said. "You *have* to. I can't be the MVP if I'm not playing in the finals, and I have to get into that USC program."

"The Blue Sox should win."

"We *should*, but look what almost happened in the quarterfinals."

"But I got my groove now, and the team? They all had a scare. No one's going to take the next game lightly. Trust me, Sam," Trevor said, "I will not let you down on Saturday."

"You should be fine. We beat Sherman Oaks before by five runs." Sam spoke as if he were thinking out loud.

"Nothing gets past RJ, I'll tell you that," Trevor said, "and as much as I can't stand him, Klum can pitch."

"Cole Price, too."

"Yes, and everyone can hit."

"People say they haven't seen a team like the Blue Sox in ten years, but don't even ask to pinch-hit for me in the finals. That's where I have to shine. That's when the USC coaches will be there. That's everything to me."

"I won't," Trevor said.

Sam hesitated for a second, not certain he wanted to hear the answer to his next question. "So, you like being me?"

"Most of it. What about being me?"

"What's not to like?" Sam said.

"If I could play baseball, it'd be pretty perfect."

"My dad says nothing's perfect," Sam said.

"That's funny," Trevor said. "Mine, too."

"Hey, what happens when you go to the beach house? Do the servants bring your clothes and toothbrush and stuff?"

"Naw, it's all there, everything you need."

"You have two of everything?"

"I guess."

"Oh, okay. That makes sense."

"Question for you," Trevor said. "Is there any way I can get out of tagging along with your dad to his studio appointments next week?"

"Just . . . stay home. If you want. Tell him your nose is stuffed up."

"Sounds good."

"It gets pretty rank smelling during the day; that's why you'll want to mention your nose. I wouldn't stay there all day in the summer unless I couldn't smell." Sam looked out over the ocean and shook his head at the difference in their lives.

"That's no big deal."

"Really? You know, you might be able to talk him into leaving you at the batting cage, but make sure you bring a book. He'll never believe I'd sit there all day without a book."

"You got it. Hey, I gotta go; your dad just gave me a shout. Dinner's ready."

Sam said good-bye and hung up the phone. He watched Trevor's parents for a minute sitting on the terrace below him, listening to the surf. When Thomas, the butler, appeared between them and said something, Trevor's dad finished his wine and kissed Trevor's mom. He suddenly looked up and caught Sam staring.

Instead of a frown, Trevor's dad broke out into a glowing white grin and gave Sam a thumbs-up. Sam smiled and offered his own thumbs-up before Trevor's dad disappeared inside the house.

Sam knew in his heart that Trevor was wrong. No question Trevor's dad was an intimidating figure. He was like a lion. The power he possessed seemed to ooze from every inch of his body. But the ferociousness was for outsiders. Sam felt as safe as he did with his own father, safer, even. His gut told him that Trevor's dad, tough as he might be in business, was a reasonable man who'd understand what Sam and Trevor were doing, and why.

He just knew Trevor's dad would want to help, and he knew things would be a lot easier that way, too. After all, the deal was that Sam got to use his role to get a green light for his dad.

Wouldn't coming clean with Trevor's dad be the very best way to make that happen? Rather than dancing around the edges of things with Stu and working through McKenna, Sam just knew how easy it would all be if Trevor's dad was involved. The man could literally snap his fingers and make it happen.

Sam went back into Trevor's bedroom and put on a pair of jeans since the night had begun to cool. He poked his head out into the hallway and listened. Voices came from the office Trevor's father had interviewed Moffit in earlier. Sam snuck down the stairs and stopped outside to listen. Trevor's dad was talking with someone who sounded like a smoker. The voice was low and rough, and he coughed after nearly every sentence. Sam looked around at the empty entryway, then moved closer to the door.

He scanned the area again before putting his ear to the crack.

"I don't care!" Trevor's father yelled.

Sam jumped, but put his ear right back to the crack.

"Gerry, come on. How long have you known Sherm? Didn't you two make your first film together?"

Trevor's dad remained silent.

"He named his oldest son after you," the smoker said before coughing.

"Art, you listen to me and listen carefully." Trevor's dad growled like a dog ready to bite. "What's the worst thing someone can do to you?"

"I don't know. Run off with your wife?"

"Deceive you. Trick you. *Lie* to you. Someone who does that is no good. This business is full of that kind of garbage.

231

I've *never* tolerated it, and I won't tolerate it now."

"Gerry, think about it. You cut him out and he loses everything, not just everything he's saved; he'll lose his house and probably his family when they find out."

"He should have thought about that before he tried to make a fool of me," Trevor's dad said.

"I don't even think he was trying to make a fool of you. He just wasn't thinking."

"Well, maybe he'll think next time. If there is a next time, which there won't be with me. Now, leave." Trevor's dad's final words ended in a snarl so low, Sam could barely hear it, but he knew what the words meant.

When the door opened, Sam fell forward and spilled into the room sprawled out on the floor.

64

SAM

The man with the rough smoker's voice gasped, but he kept his hold on the door handle. Trevor's dad rose up from behind his desk.

"Trevor! What are you doing?"

Sam scrambled to his feet and stood facing Trevor's dad. "I . . . came to ask you something. To tell you something."

Sam glanced at the other man. He was old and fat and wore a rumpled suit. He seemed out of breath.

Trevor's dad dismissed the man, who closed the door behind him.

Sam faced Trevor's father. Gone was the warm, pleasant face from earlier in the day. It seemed to Sam that the painting from the upstairs hallway had come to life.

"Well? What is it, Son?"

65

SAM

Sam sputtered a bit before he finally found the words jammed up in his throat. "I wanted to talk to you about . . . this looking for my biological mother thing. I just wanted to know if, when you find her, you could not tell her. I mean, I'd like to know who she is and where, but I don't want her to know."

Trevor's dad wrinkled his forehead. "I guess I'm not sure I understand."

Sam's head spun. "Well, I just want to know she's okay and where she is and . . . I know I'm sounding flaky, but I'm not one hundred percent sure I want to meet her."

Trevor's dad's face softened. "You caught me at a bad time. That—what you heard, me shouting—was just business. I'm sorry, but I don't trust anyone outside you and your mother, Trevor. You're all I have and you're the only people on earth I can count on.

"Anyway, I can do this however you want. We don't have to find her at all."

"No, no. I want to find her. I want to know all about her. I just . . . is it okay?"

"Of course. Here, let's go out on the terrace with your mom. Let's enjoy each other's company and have dinner, and we can watch an old movie or something."

Sam realized he'd been holding his breath and he let it out as he followed Trevor's dad out onto the terrace. It surprised him that even the presence of Trevor's father didn't keep the mother from texting and talking on the phone all through dinner as if Sam and the father weren't there, but she did. They had grilled lobsters, and Sam didn't know if he'd ever tasted anything so good. He was surprised to learn that Trevor's father knew almost everything about the Dodgers, and that's what the two of them talked about—including the "scrimmage" Trevor played on his birthday—until they'd finished their ice cream sundaes and Trevor's mom suggested he get to bed.

Sam didn't argue, even though, with the candlelit dinner and the billowing white canopy over their table, the terrace seemed like a magical place—one that he didn't really want to leave. He took a shower and opened the glass doors so the breeze could blow in. In the bookcase were leather bound copies of the classics. Sam was pleased to find *The Count of Monte Cristo*. He found the spot where he'd gotten to in his book at home and switched on the lamp next to the bed before settling down.

He had no idea what time it was when Trevor's father knocked gently. The Hollywood mogul entered the room wearing a thick robe and sat on the edge of the bed. He stared at

Sam for a moment with a small smile on his face.

"What?" Sam asked.

Trevor's father pointed to the book. "I love that. When did you decide to start reading?"

Sam shifted under the covers. "I don't know."

"Do you like it?"

"It's okay."

"Okay? Where are you? Has Edmond escaped from prison?"

"Yes. He just won the knife fight."

"Ah, the knife fight. He's become a brutal man, right?"

"I guess most people would."

"Of course. Betrayal. That would make anyone brutal. It's human nature. Well, I'm impressed. Keep it up, Trevor. You know how I feel about reading. I'm glad you finally found out on your own. Good night."

Sam took the hand Trevor's father offered and shook it. When the door closed, Sam put out the light and listened to the sound of the waves. He'd come dangerously close to ruining everything, but the idea to ask that Moffit not let his mother know about him served two purposes. It was not only a good excuse for why he'd been skulking around outside the office door; it would also make Trevor happy.

Sam would have all the information he needed, and he could take it with him. Trevor could simply say he'd become certain he didn't want to meet his mother. Then when Sam was safely back with his father, he could contact her on his own. It was perfect. The only thing he needed to do now was hope Moffit could get the information in the next week. Sam let himself dream about his mother for a few minutes, who she might be, what, and where, but that led back to when and why. Why was not something Sam wanted to think about because it brought him full circle to Trevor and the anger he felt.

"Are you angry?" Sam whispered the words out loud. They seemed to slip past his lips like snakes in the grass. "Are you, Sam?"

That was something he didn't want to think about. So, when Trevor's phone buzzed and he saw it was McKenna asking if he could call her, Sam happily dialed her up.

"Hey," Sam said when she answered.

"You sound down," McKenna said, "but I bet you won't be when you hear what I'm going to tell you."

Trevor didn't want to go back.

He had to admit that to himself. He had helped to win the league game Tuesday night, spent most days at the cage, then evenings practicing with his team—that's how he thought of it now, as *his* team—and after that, hanging out with Sam's dad. Sam's dad was something Trevor hadn't expected. Sam's dad asked questions, and *listened* to what Trevor said. And after Sam's dad listened, he'd ask more questions, and then Trevor would ask questions he'd never thought of before, and they'd end up just talking until late.

Trevor never would have believed just talking like that until late at night was possible. The one thing he was determined to do—no matter what was happening to the project when he returned to his old life—was get Mr. Palomaki's script made into a movie. If he had to beg his own father to do it, he would. He wanted to give that to the man so bad it hurt. Trevor had seen writers and producers who were arrogant, stupid, and mean; and by gosh, if they could get their movies made, a man like Sam's dad deserved it ten times over.

But that would be for when he returned, and Trevor didn't *want* to return. The problem was—and he knew it—that the longer he was Sam Palomaki, the more he wanted to stay Sam Palomaki. Sam's life was *real*. It was a struggle, yes, but it was real and there were obstacles that had to be overcome. In Trevor's world there were no obstacles. Everything was set. It was a roller-coaster ride, no doubt. But, like every roller-coaster ride, once you did it enough, once you knew every twist, turn, and drop like your own speed dial list, the thrill was gone. This new life, on the other hand, was still a thrill.

The phone rang. It was Sam. Trevor lay on the bed and thought about not picking up. Finally, he did.

"Ready for the big game?"

"You don't know how ready," Trevor said.

Sam laughed. "Tomorrow's a big day for me, too. I've got Moffit *and* Stu. They're both coming by the set. McKenna told me last night that she thinks Stu has a lead on something."

"They didn't finish the castle scenes?" Trevor asked, knowing what happened when they got behind schedule.

"Nah. They were having trouble with the stuntmen on fire. Something about the coating on the suits and something they had in the water to make it really black. These guys were falling in the moat and the fire was spreading across the top of the water. They burned the drawbridge twice before they figured out the problem. So, we start at six a.m."

"Ouch."

"Trust me, that's not pain. You know what pain is now, right?"

Trevor asked, "What do you mean?"

"Oh, how about my dad crabbing on you about leaving dishes in the sink? Or the smell of garbage? Or taking a shower in a plastic capsule the size of a Porta-Potti? Or frozen dinners? Or having the air conditioner bog down on a hot night? All pain that you never had to experience, and won't have to experience again. Ever."

"It's not so bad," Trevor said.

"Careful, or I'll have you pinch-hitting for me for good."

Trevor's heart galloped, but then Sam laughed.

"I'm kidding," Sam said. "I miss my dad and his Shakespeare quotes. I can't say I miss the smell of the landfill, but I am looking forward to lighting up the ballpark in the finals and seeing the stupid look on Klum's face when I win the MVP and launch my career toward the Major Leagues."

"So, Stu and Moffit both tomorrow, huh?" Trevor said. "What do you think?"

"Fingers crossed with Stu. You don't want to know about Moffit, really, do you?"

"No," Trevor said, "not really. I was just thinking about you is all."

Sam said, "I appreciate that."

"Why didn't Moffit just text you the information?"

"Your dad told him no paper and no electronics. He doesn't

240

want this getting out. He said everything has to be verbal. I don't know; it sounds a little paranoid to me, but it's not my money, right?"

Silence sat between them like a third person on the call.

Sam finally said, "Do you think we can be friends after this? I don't know, hang out sometimes?"

"You know," Trevor said, "I was thinking the same thing yesterday. Honestly? I don't think so. I think we were lucky to get away with all this. It was great for me, and I hope it's been great for you. Part of me doesn't want to go back. But I know I will. I have to, and I know the best thing for both of us is to let it go. I don't know how your dad would be, but I'll tell you that if mine found out, he'd undo anything Stu can get done with your dad's script. That I can promise you.

"On the other hand, maybe your dad's movie is a hit and you and me are able to meet normally and—who knows—maybe we work together, or maybe we even play baseball."

"And your mom? How would she fit into this?" Sam asked. "She freaked out when she saw me on set."

"My mom, yes. She'd be a problem. Let's not think about it. Let's just enjoy the last day and a half we've got, don't you think? I mean, I gotta believe you're going to miss McKenna, right?"

"McKenna?" Sam's voice fell.

"You can't take her with you," Trevor said, trying to be funny.

"Well, she and I can still be friends. There's no reason we can't."

"Really? Okay. I'm not arguing." Trevor knew by Sam's tone that he'd struck a nerve.

"Why did you say that, though?" Sam asked. "What's McKenna got to do with all this?"

"McKenna's part of my world, right? Like baseball is part of yours." Trevor spoke patiently to try and ease the pain. "You gotta take the good with the bad, Sam. That's what your dad says."

"My dad doesn't know everything." Sam sounded more upset by the moment.

"Look, I don't want to fight. McKenna's great. Maybe you guys can work something out, right?" Trevor tried to add real hope to his voice, but it was just acting.

"I like her, Trevor. I like her more than you ever did."

"Yeah, I guess I know that, Sam," Trevor said, losing patience. "That's good. I hope it works out."

"Why shouldn't it?" Sam's voice rose.

"Sam, don't yell at me. I'm not the one who makes the rules. I hope it works out, okay? I mean that, but it seems like it could be tough. She's kind of a star, Sam."

"And I'm nothing? I'm going to play for the Dodgers, *really play*, not some make-believe nonsense!"

Trevor nodded to himself. He liked Sam's confidence. It reminded him of his own. Still, the conversation was going nowhere.

"Hey, Sam. I gotta go. Enjoy yourself, buddy. I got a game tomorrow. See you at the party on Sunday."

"Fine."

Sam hung up, and Trevor stared at the phone for a minute

before plugging it in to charge and setting it on the night table. He turned off the light and lay there for a minute before snapping it back on and picking up the phone. Sam's emotional reaction was something he didn't think would be good to ignore.

"McKenna?" Trevor said when she answered. "I think we got a problem."

67
SAM

Sam didn't sleep well.

When he woke, he remembered tossing and turning until well after midnight. The alarm busted him loose from a pleasant dream. He and McKenna were flying in the helicopter, but when they got to the beach house, they decided to just keep going, all the way to Tahiti. Sam wasn't completely sure where Tahiti was, but that didn't matter in the dream. McKenna thought it was a good idea, and that was all that had mattered.

Sam yawned and staggered to the bathroom. He took as cold a shower as he could stand and threw on some shorts along with a Kobe Bryant Lakers jersey, signed, of course. Gabriel looked tired, too, and when Sam flopped down in the back of the limo, Gabriel barely squeaked out a "Good morning." Only Dolph and Wolf, sitting up front, looked alert. Sam offered nothing more than a nod of his head as a greeting to Gabriel, annoyed that the dream had faded so quickly and afraid that his time with McKenna was dissolving like a bread crust in acid—a science experiment he remembered from school.

Before he knew it, they pulled into the studio lot, a ghost town on Saturday without cars or people. The hulking airplane hangar buildings lay like giants sleeping in rows. Sam left Gabriel behind, practically dashing for his dressing room. McKenna sat waiting. Her eyes were red.

Sam sat next to her on the couch and took her hand. "Were you crying?"

"No," she said, shaking her head. "Yes. It's been fun, that's all. Tomorrow everything changes. I didn't want to have this stupid pool party to begin with."

"There's no reason we can't still hang out," Sam said.

She nodded ferociously, as if someone had told her otherwise. "Today's a big day, right? Stu and Moffit both reporting in. No thanks to Sara Grant, though. I still can't believe she ratted you out."

"We've been through this a hundred times," Sam said. "It all worked out fine."

Sam hesitated. "You still haven't answered me, though. We can hang out after tomorrow, right?"

"Don't mind me, Sam. I just don't trust the grown-ups. They have all these rules about who can do what, when, and with who."

"My dad's pretty lax on rules."

"Mine isn't." McKenna hopped up from the couch. "But that doesn't matter. We've got today, right?"

"You sound like you were talking to Trevor." Sam stared at

245

her, but she would only look away and nod. "Is he right? He said you and I can't be friends after this, but why not? I can visit. You can even come to my games."

"Maybe we can," she said, but her words were lighter than smoke and they floated away without real meaning. McKenna pointed to Sam's neck. "Come on, let me touch up that birthmark a bit before makeup gets here. It's fading a little, and we'll start soon. I saw Pierce Everette with his coffee, and once he's got his coffee, things move fast."

Sam bit his lip, and things did move fast. They shot three scenes with Sam making quick changes and muffing his lines enough that it seemed they were already behind schedule by ten in the morning. When they finally took a break for the crew, Sam returned to his dressing room. As he changed, he fished Trevor's phone out of his jeans only to find the red light blinking.

McKenna came in before he could check the messages. "Sam, Stu just got here. He's talking to Pierce, but he'll be right in. Is something wrong?"

"I don't know." Sam felt light-headed at the mention of Stu because he knew the news would be big either way. He examined the phone. "I've got thirteen missed calls, all from Trevor."

McKenna's smile went out. "Then something *is* wrong."

A knock at the dressing room door startled them both. McKenna flung it open. Sam expected Stu, but the face that appeared belonged to someone else.

68

TREVOR

Trevor woke with the birds and used fresh makeup to cover his birthmark and lighten his skin color a bit. In the mirror, he looked for signs of worry in his face. This was not only the last game he'd get to play, it was the one that could make or break Sam's dreams. He wished he could play next week in the Tuesday night game and the tournament finals as well, but he knew Sam would never go for that. The finals were where Sam had to make his mark, get that MVP and a spot with USC. Even today's game was important, and while he talked a good game with Sam about the semifinals being a cakewalk, Trevor knew he had to perform well.

Finished, he shuffled out of the trailer in the early dawn light, shivered, and blew into his hands. The garbage smell had been tamped down by the cool air. His feet scuffed along

247

the gravel road. He had to walk, had to move to keep from going crazy with nerves. Most of it was excitement, but he had to admit there was a healthy amount of fear mixed in, too. As well as he'd done in practice and his first league game last Tuesday, he still sensed that he wasn't quite up to Sam's level.

By the time Trevor got back, Sam's dad was awake. Eggs sizzled and spit in the pan.

"Everything okay?" Sam's dad asked over his shoulder.

"Antsy, that's all." Trevor sat down.

They ate in silence off paper plates. Trevor asked if they could head out early to spend some time at the batting cage.

"You're not overdoing it, are you?"

Trevor hesitated. "I've been a little off is all. Maybe it will help."

"You're a little off. Not too bad. That happens. Even the Major Leaguers get into slumps. You'll climb out of it."

Trevor's heart sank when he heard Sam's dad say the word "slump."

"Hey, come on. You will."

Trevor bit the side of his cheek and looked away. Sam's dad cleaned up. Trevor helped, then got Sam's bat bag from the bedroom. They rode to the cages in silence, the Ferrari sputtering to a halt in the parking lot.

Trevor worked hard, swinging and connecting like a machine. He and Sam's dad arrived at the ballpark early with the rest of the team for a light batting practice. They had only just begun when Coach Sharp blew his whistle and called them all in to the dugout. Beside him stood a man Trevor didn't recognize.

"Guys, this is Coach Blasi. He's the batting coach at USC."

Trevor felt his jaw go slack.

"Guys, I know you thought we'd be making our Elite Training Center selections at the championship next week, but Coach Cruz got invited to an Olympic Committee meeting in China next week, so we're going to make our choices today." Coach Blasi was young, with a brush cut and pale green eyes. He spoke softly. "We'll choose one player from the winning team in your game and do the same thing for the other semifinal game tomorrow. We're sorry if this throws you off at all, but we did want you to know that today is the day."

For a minute Trevor could only just sit there, even as the rest of the Blue Sox poured back out onto the field. Dread sat heavy in the pit of his stomach. He had to get Sam. As much as he wanted to play, he knew it was unlikely he'd play well enough to win the MVP, and now that that decision was being made today instead of next week in the finals, Trevor *knew* that somehow, some way, he had to switch back with Sam.

"Sam!" Coach Sharp shouted from the infield.

"Coming, Coach!" With trembling fingers, Trevor unzipped Sam's bat bag and removed the phone. He quickly dialed his own number, holding Sam's phone at his side so it couldn't be seen, urging Sam to pick up. If he did, Trevor would fake sickness and run off the field to the bathroom. But Sam didn't answer, so Trevor took his place in line for a ball toss drill to hit lobbed-up balls into the backstop for timing.

249

As he stood, Trevor pocket-dialed Sam, listening to the faint ringing for an answer but getting none. Frankie got in line behind Trevor and nudged him before signaling with a shake of his head that Trevor better stop with the phone.

"Are you crazy?" Frankie rolled his eyes toward Coach Sharp.

But Trevor kept dialing.

He had to.

69
SAM

The person at the dressing room door was Moffit. He stepped inside the door wearing an expression on his face that Sam couldn't read. Suddenly he found it hard to breathe. "Just tell me who my mom is. Where is she? Do you have a phone number?"

Moffit only stared at Sam and shook his head.

"What do you mean no?" Sam's voice rose to a hysterical pitch. Everything was crazy. "You said you had news to tell me."

Finally, Moffit said, "I'm sorry, Trevor. I hate to tell you this."

70

SAM

Moffit closed the door behind him. Sam's head was already spinning at the thought of Stu's news and the fact that it looked like something was wrong with Trevor. The idea that he was about to find out something bad about his mother made his stomach drop like a bowling ball.

"Maybe sit down," Moffit said.

Sam sat, and McKenna plunked down beside him and grabbed his knee.

Moffit angled his head at McKenna. "I think maybe we should talk alone."

"McKenna can listen," Sam said.

Moffit nodded, then coughed and cleared his throat. He swallowed so that his stony Adam's apple bobbed up and down. "I can't find her, Trevor. No one can."

"What's that mean?" Sam asked.

"Just what I said. She can't be found."

Sam twisted up his face, shaking his head in disbelief at Moffit's arrogance. "Because you can't find her, no one can?"

Moffit looked at McKenna with sadness in his eyes before turning them back onto Sam. "No. She's gone, Trevor. She's dead."

Sam barely heard the hiss as McKenna drew a breath through her teeth.

"How?" he asked, his voice barely a whisper.

"Having you. In the hospital." Moffit opened his mouth, hesitated, then spoke. "There's something more."

"My father?" Sam asked.

Moffit shook his head. "No, there's no record of your father, and your mother didn't tell anyone, but you have a brother, Trevor, a twin."

Sam held up his hand. "Did you tell . . . my father this?"

Moffit shook his head. "Your father told me to give the information to you and you alone. He said it was your decision on what to do with it."

"And you won't tell anyone else?"

Moffit shook his head. "Not if you don't want me to. Your father was very specific. He said the information belonged to you alone. I have a reputation. Without that, I'd have to choose another profession."

"Okay. Thanks." Sam stood and walked Moffit to the door. When the detective was gone, Sam just stood and stared.

McKenna got up and put an arm around his shoulder, giving

him a sideways hug. "I'm sorry," she said.

Sam staggered back to the couch and dropped down onto it. "She's gone."

McKenna followed him and took his hand, squeezing it tight. "I'm so sorry, Sam."

Sam pinched his eyes shut and tears streamed down his face. He sniffed and shook his head. "It's okay. It's my own fault. I should have left it alone."

McKenna patted his shoulder.

"The boy without a mother," Sam said.

"You have a great father," McKenna said. "And you have me."

Sam opened his eyes. "For what? Another day?"

She smiled. "You'll have me after that, Sam. We're friends. We'll always be friends."

"You're a movie star."

"Well, you're going to be a baseball star."

Sam took a deep and ragged breath. "Yeah, as long as Trevor wins that game."

McKenna pointed to the phone Sam still held in his hand. "I know this is a lot for you, but if something's wrong, maybe you should call him."

71

TREVOR

When the phone vibrated, Coach Sharp was in the middle of his pep talk.

Trevor jumped up from the bench and sprinted out of the dugout.

"Bathroom," he said as he darted past the coach. "Sorry, Coach."

As soon as he rounded the corner, Trevor answered the phone and told Sam to hang on. He ran straight to the bathroom and locked himself inside a stall.

Whispering, he said, "Sam, you've got to get here."

"What? What are you talking about?"

"The game! Today is the day! USC is here! Now. They're naming MVPs from the *semifinals,* not the finals this year."

"Are you serious?"

"Of course I am. Coach Cruz has to go to China or

255

something. You think I want this? You've got to hurry. You've got to get here."

"How?" Sam practically shouted. "How do I do that? How can we switch? I can't just walk out of here."

"You have to."

"I know I have to, but tell me how."

The bathroom door squeaked open, and Trevor knew he wasn't alone. He covered the phone and his mouth. "McKenna. Tell McKenna."

Shoes scuffed to a halt just outside the stall, and there was a sharp rap of knuckles against the door.

"Sam?" Coach Sharp growled. "Sam. Open up."

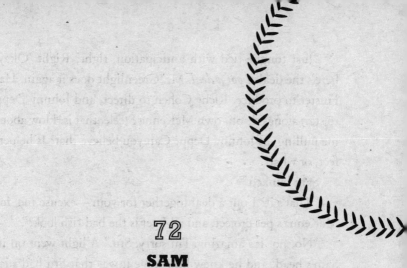

72

SAM

Sam forgot about Stu and his news about *Dark Cellar*, and even about Moffit and his mother. All he could think about was getting to the ballpark, and it made his head spin.

That didn't keep Stu from barging into the dressing room before Sam could even explain to McKenna what was going on.

"Kid! Have I been working overtime for you."

Sam stared at him.

"Can't believe it, right?" Stu scooped up a handful of Skittles from the bowl on the coffee table and dribbled a few into his mouth. "Me neither, but I told you you were my star and you are. So, you ready?"

Sam looked at McKenna.

"What's a matter? You eat some bad lox this morning? I told them, only fresh lox for my star. What's the problem?"

Sam could only shake his head.

"Just tongue-tied with anticipation, right? Right. Okay, here's the deal: *I got a deal.* Mr. Greenlight does it again. Hal Finster to produce, Richy Cohen to direct, and Johnny Depp to star, alongside our own McKenna Steele, that is. How about me pulling off Johnny Depp? Can you believe that? Is he perfect, or what?"

Sam blinked.

"That's it? I put a deal together for your—excuse me, for McKenna's pet project, and all I get is the bad-fish look?"

"No, no. It's amazing. I'm sorry, Stu." A light went on in Sam's head, and he knew how huge it was that Stu had succeeded, one of his father's scripts finally being made into a movie after twelve years. But the glare of the news about his mother and the thought of missing out on USC made the green light seem like a blip.

"You *should* be sorry." Stu's lower lip stuck out. "Mr. Greenlight is a magician. He's a Hollywood master, a maestro, a maestro master, that's what he is."

"It's unbelievable, Stu. Really unbelievable," McKenna said.

"Now, there's a young lady with some sense. She knows what's what." Stu grinned at her.

"But I gotta go." Sam couldn't help saying the words; they just came out.

Stu stared for a minute, then shook his head. He laughed bitterly, then chuckled to himself. He flicked a hand in the air as he muttered on his way out of the dressing room. "The kid is a chip off the old man's ice-cold block of a heart."

The door slammed shut.

"Sam?" McKenna wore a pained expression.

Sam shared Trevor's news with her.

McKenna looked horrified. "Then we've got to get you there."

"How, McKenna, *how*?" Sam felt fresh tears building up in the corners of his eyes.

McKenna's eyes sparkled and she raised her jaw.

"Follow me."

73

TREVOR

Trevor whipped his pants down, tucked the phone into his underwear, and sat down. Coach Sharp rapped again.

"Sam?"

Trevor leaned forward and flicked the latch. The coach stuck his head around the corner of the door and immediately looked away. "What are you doing?"

Trevor conjured up a groan. "Coach, my stomach. I think I ate something."

"You ate something, or you called someone?"

Trevor stayed quiet for a moment. "What are you talking about?"

"What are *you* talking about, on that phone? I heard you in there."

Trevor thought fast. "I called my dad for some toilet paper, Coach."

"You don't have any?"

"No, Coach."

Trevor heard the coach sigh through the door and then go into the next stall, where he rolled off some paper before handing it under the door. "You've been real squirrelly this week, I gotta say. If you want any chance at USC Elite, you gotta snap out of it. You know what I mean?"

"I do, Coach."

"Okay. Do what you got to and get out there."

"You got it, Coach."

74
SAM

"Give me thirty seconds," McKenna said. "I'll distract Gabriel. You head for the back and make your first right. There's a hallway that leads outside to some picnic tables; the crew uses it as a smoking area. Don't say anything to anyone, and don't look at them. You just walk right by. If anyone asks you any questions, just hold your hand up like they shouldn't talk to you, like you're upset. When you get outside, take a hard left. Go all the way to the back of this building. There's all these crates and barrels back there stacked against the wall. Tuck in there, and I'll come get you."

"Tuck in?"

"Hide."

"For how long?"

McKenna shrugged. "Hopefully not long at all. When does the game start?"

262

"Eleven o'clock."

McKenna looked at her watch and blew some air past her lips. "I've got to figure out who I can trust."

"Well, we know it's not Sara Grant."

"I know that, and we know it's *not* Gabriel."

"Yes, but who?" Sam wrinkled his forehead, then snapped his fingers. "Dolph, that's who."

"Dolph? Your driver? He barely speaks English."

"He'll do it, trust me. You tell him it's for me. You tell him I said he can return the favor."

"What favor?" McKenna asked.

"Does that matter now? Trust me," Sam said.

"Okay," McKenna said, "it's your scholarship, or whatever it is. Here we go."

75

SAM

Sam waited, counting as slow as he could to thirty before he peeked around the dressing room door. McKenna not only had Gabriel distracted, she was leading him away. Sam darted down the hallway and took his first right. He burst out of the door into the sunlight and did exactly what McKenna told him to do. He kept his eyes straight ahead, looking at no one, and no one said a word.

When he rounded the corner, his heart skipped a beat. He looked over his shoulder. No one had followed him. He ducked between two barrels, rounded a big crate, and slipped inside. The pile of junk overhead was tall enough so that only small threads of light leaked through. In the darkness Sam could hear his own heartbeat. He strained his ears for the sound of Dolph's car.

When he finally did hear something, it wasn't a car.

It was footsteps.

They rounded the corner, scuffing grit. Sam heard heavy breathing, and then Gabriel's voice.

"Trevor . . . or whoever you are . . . you might as well come out.

"The game is up."

76

TREVOR

Trevor stepped down into the dugout. Coach Sharp stared at him. Trevor shook his head and held his stomach. Coach Sharp pinched his lips tight and shook his head.

"Can you warm up?" the coach asked.

"Yes." Trevor slipped on his glove and stepped out onto the field, taking his place at shortstop.

He felt Coach Sharp's eyes on him as he scooped up a grounder in the pepper drill. He made the throw to first and nodded to Frankie as the ball smacked into his glove. Trevor checked behind the backstop and saw the USC coach watching him. He punched his empty glove and got into a ready position, but he couldn't help grinning. He knew if Sam didn't make it back, he'd never be able to win the MVP on his own, but there was another option.

If Sam made it back *partway* through the game, all Trevor

had to do in the meantime was not mess things up. If he could play without any major errors and not look horrible at the plate, maybe he could just hang on until Sam got here to make some stupendous plays that would earn him the MVP. It wasn't a great plan, but under the circumstances, it was the best thing Trevor could come up with. Because the Blue Sox were the home team, the visitors from Sherman Oaks would bat first.

If Sam could somehow get a ride out to the ballpark right away, he might be there within thirty minutes. With only fifteen minutes to go before the game started, Trevor knew he'd have to fill in for Sam at least one inning in the field. If Sam *could* get out there right away, then Trevor *might* not have to bat.

That's what he had to hope for.

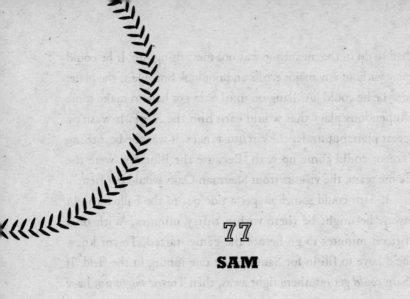

77

SAM

Sam's stomach heaved and sweat beaded his brow.

He licked his lips but stayed put, frozen with fear, not so much of Gabriel finding him, but of what would happen next. In that split second he could see it all: his father caught in a scandal with the green light put out forever. The story in the papers, Trevor's life being thrown into chaos, his father sent to jail, and him probably being tossed into a foster home without a prayer of seeing McKenna ever again.

A phone rang—Gabriel's.

"Yes, I'm in the back. . . . Because someone saw him come back this way, that's why. There's a jungle of crates and boxes back here and—

"Who said that? McKenna did? I'll be right there."

Gabriel's footsteps pounded away, skidding around the corner of the studio and fading to nothing.

Sam didn't know if he should stay or go.

Trevor's phone buzzed in his pocket, startling him. He took it out and read the text from McKenna.

can u get thru th fence?
if ys we cn mt u on road
thru trees

Sam slipped out of the crate and peered between the barrels. The fence stood ten feet high. On top were three strands of barbed wire, strung the entire length as far as Sam could see on metal struts pointing out and up at an angle away from the top of the fence. Beyond the fence the line of trees was too thick to see the road, but if McKenna said it was there, Sam believed her. He poked his head out from between the barrels, scanning side to side. There was nothing to see but boxes, barrels, broken pavement, and the back of the next studio.

He stepped out and approached the fence. As he looked to his left, he saw that beyond the next building the fence turned at a ninety-degree angle, heading back toward the buildings. In that corner was a small V-shaped space between the strands of barbed wire where one section ended and another began. Sam texted as he ran, telling McKenna that he thought he'd found a way.

When he passed the open area between the two giant buildings, he glanced that way and saw a handful of people on the opposite end. Sam didn't bother to see whether they'd spotted him or not, he just kept running. When he hit the corner of the fence, he leaped up and clung to the thick wire links. By jamming the tips of his toes into the small holes of the fence, he was able to climb to the top. When he reached the top, he realized the V-shaped opening in the barbed wire was narrower than he thought, and would require him to get sideways to pass through it.

The sound of voices shouting Trevor's name echoed off the far studio wall, moving toward him. Sam gripped the strut where the barbed wire ended and used it to help steady himself as he eased a leg through the gap. His heart banged around on the inside of his chest like a pinball. With one leg through, he twisted around so he faced the studio.

The shouts grew closer still, just around the corner. Sam panicked and swung his other leg up and over the barbed wire instead of taking the time to turn sideways and slip it through the gap.

The cuff of his jeans caught hold.

The barb bit into his ankle.

Sam jerked backward, lost his grip, and fell. The pant leg snagged by the wire yanked at him and he bounced, swinging upside down, suspended by the wire.

One of the voices turned into a scream. Sam was vaguely aware of the people shouting and screaming from the other side of the fence. He was distracted by the rocky ground nearly ten feet below and a sound much more terrifying than a simple scream. In all the ruckus, Sam could hear only one noise.

The rip and tear of his pants.

78

TREVOR

Sherman Oaks had one run already. There was a man on first, but one more out would end the inning. Butterflies continued to flutter in Trevor's stomach, even though they were well into the first inning. Part of his nervousness was because he couldn't decide if he wanted the ball to come to him or not. So far he'd only clapped for their pitcher, Tommy Graham, on two strikeouts and watched as two balls sailed overhead, one outside the park and a second into right field that left the runner on first.

Trevor checked his watch. He ached to know where Sam was. Graham wound up and threw a strike. The runner on first started to steal. Trevor bolted to second, ready for the throw from home plate. It came like a missile, and all Trevor could think of was that he could not miss it. Of all the things in his life he'd ever flubbed, this could not be one of them. From the corner of his eye, he saw the runner stop halfway down the baseline and go back.

The ball snapped into Trevor's glove, and without thinking he flung the ball to first. It was smooth and relaxed, and the throw was perfect.

SNAP.

The ball hit the first baseman's glove, low and a bit outside so that Frankie could sweep his glove across and tag the runner. The runner slid. Frankie tagged his leg.

The umpire behind the plate shouted, "Safe."

The Blue Sox fans groaned and booed the close call.

Trevor still trembled but couldn't contain the smile on his face. He'd done just what he needed to do, and the play he'd made would only help Sam's stock with the USC coaches. He relaxed, straightening for a moment while Frankie tossed the ball back to Graham. Trevor returned to his position and settled his weight over the balls of his feet, bouncing ever so slightly and ready to go.

He still wore his mad grin when Graham wound up and delivered a fastball right down the middle. The bat cracked and the ball was a blur heading for the open space between him and the third baseman on a low line. In the millisecond it shot through the infield, several things went through Trevor's mind.

First, he knew it would take incredible skill and a near miracle to snag the line drive. Second, if he dove for it and missed, he would be out of position if the ball got past the left fielder and he needed a cutoff man to keep the runner from rounding third and scoring. The safe thing was to stay on his feet and provide a cutoff.

However, he knew if he *did* make the play, it would be spectacular and he would be *helping* Sam, rather than not hurting him, and it would help the team *win*. That might have been the most exciting prospect of all, and it was what took over his body and mind—the desire to win. So, with a burst of adrenaline, hunger, and joy, Trevor launched himself into the air, stretching every fiber toward the ball.

79
SAM

As the pants gave way, Sam swung himself like an acrobat, flexing his hips out, then in. As the pants tore free from the barbed wire, he reached out and snatched a grip on the chain-link fence, first with one hand, then the other. His legs dropped below him and his fingers spun around the insides of the holes he gripped so that he clung now to the fence, facing the onrushing handful of people from the movie set.

Without a second thought, Sam let himself drop the remaining three or four feet to the ground. His feet slipped, and he tumbled and rolled into the bushes. Then, slithering like a snake, he bellied his way into the trees, where he rose up and took off at a full sprint away from the fence and the studio and the horrified people crying out for "Trevor" to come back.

Sam broke through the trees and stumbled down a small slope, losing his balance and tumbling again, this time into a dry ditch. As he crawled up out of it, he could hear the racing sound of an engine. He poked his head up and saw a car rocketing toward him. The glare of sunlight off the windshield told him nothing about the driver, but the car looked like a big limo. It screeched to a halt alongside him, and the rear passenger door swung open.

80

SAM

Sitting in the backseat and waving him into the limo was McKenna.

Sam jumped in and pulled the door shut.

"Go, Dolph."

The car took off. Sam buckled up, and McKenna did the same.

"Mr. Trevor," Dolph said in his heavy accent. "You tell me where we go."

Sam gave Dolph directions to the ballpark and thanked Dolph for coming through. "I hope you don't get into trouble."

"Mr. Gabriel, he very angry," Dolph said, shaking his head and clucking his tongue. "But I owe favor, Mr. Trevor. I hope no lose job."

"You won't lose your job if I have anything to do with it," Sam said.

Dolph smiled and stepped on the gas.

Sam turned to McKenna. "How'd you get away?"

"It was easy. Everyone's in an uproar." McKenna was clearly delighted. "I told them you were upset and talking about quitting. I told them you were having personal problems I couldn't discuss. It was like I kicked a hornet's nest. Everyone was swarming all over the place looking for you. I got into the car and told Dolph you needed him. We just drove right out of the studio and came around the back. It's perfect. Here, let me put some makeup on that phony birthmark. We've got to cover it up."

Sam nodded, impressed with how thorough and smart McKenna was as she dusted up his neck. Then he thought of something and said, "But what about the switch?"

"Switch?"

"Trevor and I have to trade places." Sam looked at the time on his phone. "The game's already started."

McKenna frowned. "Well, your dad's script is already a done deal, and this game is more important to you than people finding out about you pinch-hitting for each other, right? I mean, it'll make a mess, but it might even be *good* for your dad's script. Everyone will be talking about it."

Sam shook his head. "Don't you get it? The game *started*. Trevor is out there playing already. If they find out we made a switch, I'll be disqualified. There's no way I get the MVP. There's no way they'll even let me play. You can't substitute players in the middle of a game. No one can know."

81

TREVOR

Thunk.

It might have been the sweetest thing Trevor had ever felt. Even as he crashed to the dirt, jarring his joints and bones, his body flushed with delight. The ball sat snug in his glove. The crowd in the stands went absolutely wild. Trevor's teammates swarmed him. They thumped his back and mussed his hair. They hugged him, and RJ kissed his cheek.

Trevor's face burned from the thrill and the embarrassment and the pride.

He jogged to the dugout, dusting himself off. Coach Sharp gripped his hand with an iron shake. "That's the Sam I know."

Trevor opened his mouth, then stopped. It scared him how close he'd come to telling Coach Sharp that he wasn't Sam, he was Trevor Goldman, and Trevor Goldman was the one who'd made the spectacular play.

Instead he looked down and muttered, "Thanks, Coach."

The excitement quickly faded because they were down by one run and the Sherman Oaks pitcher was a boy no one had seen before. According to the roster, his name was Lee Pitts. His father had been a pro football player, and his arm was strong. The balls he threw warming up snapped into the catcher's mitt like gunshots.

"Look at his arm action," RJ said. "It's practically sidearm. Thank God he's not throwing curves."

The next pitch was a curve. RJ winced. Trevor knew what it meant. It meant that when Pitts threw a curve, it would look like it was coming right at you, then curve away at the last second. Most curveballs were twelve-six, where the ball started high and curved down. This pitcher would be a nightmare.

Coach Sharp stood right in front of where Trevor sat. The coach leaned over and spoke into the ear of one of his assistants. "Where'd this kid come from?"

The other coach shrugged and leafed through some papers and pointed. "Here, he's been hurt. That's why we didn't see him when we scouted these guys, but he was on the roster earlier in the year."

"Oh boy," Coach Sharp said as another pitch smacked the catcher's mitt. "We're in for it."

Dorian Klum sat two players down from Trevor, and he leaned over to Scotty Needum and said, "Good thing they're picking MVPs today. I can hit this guy, but I doubt these other schmucks can."

Trevor's butterflies returned. He watched in horror as RJ, their first batter today, jumped away from a curve that the umpire called a strike when he was already 0–2. Frankie walked to the plate and Trevor left his seat to warm up. As he swung, he watched Frankie.

Pitts wound up and threw and Frankie jumped back.

"Strike!" The umpire held up a finger.

Frankie's face reddened, embarrassed by the fright he'd had at getting hit when the pitch crossed the center of the plate. Frankie hung in and swung on the next two pitches, nicking the second one to stay alive. Pitts threw a fastball and Frankie connected. The ball took off down the third-base line but veered foul.

Frankie stepped out of the box, took a practice swing, and stepped back in.

Coach Sharp stepped up beside Trevor and they watched together as Frankie flinched at another curveball.

"Strike three!" The umpire pumped his thumb toward the stands.

Frankie grit his teeth and shook his head, stomping back toward the dugout.

"You know what you gotta do, right, Sam?" Coach Sharp asked.

"Get a hit."

"Funny, but you know what I mean, right?"

Trevor looked at the coach in confusion. "I guess I don't know what you mean, Coach."

"You gotta switch-hit." Coach Sharp scowled and looked out at the Sherman Oaks pitcher. "You line up and bat lefty and you neutralize that curveball. I'm just glad you can hit from both sides of the plate."

Trevor closed his mouth tight and swallowed the bile churning up from his stomach. He had no idea how he'd keep from throwing up. His brain swam in a sea of fog, and his feet seemed to float up off the ground.

Even in the batting cage, Trevor had never hit lefty in his life.

82

SAM

Dolph pulled up into the entrance of Elysian Park. McKenna leaned over to the window and tilted her head to look up at the sky.

"What are you looking at?" Sam looked up, too.

"Wishing for rain. If it rained and the game got delayed, we could make the switch, easy."

"Or some kind of delay," Sam said, thinking out loud.

McKenna snapped her fingers. "Yes. A squirrel."

Sam scowled like she'd lost her mind. "Squirrel?"

McKenna's face brightened. "Remember a couple years ago, when the Yankees were playing the Twins? A squirrel ran out onto the field and stopped the game. They had to wait till it got off."

"Right, but where are we going to get a squirrel?" Sam could see the ballpark and he directed Dolph to pull up among some cars parked near the backstop behind home plate. His heart galloped at the sight of Trevor approaching the plate. He knew he might only get three or four at bats, and he couldn't afford to have Trevor blow one of them. Still, he had no idea how they could make the switch now. The squirrel idea was crazy.

"We don't have a squirrel," McKenna said, pointing toward the front seat, "but we've got a dog."

83

TREVOR

Trevor met Coach Sharp's eyes. "No, Coach. I can't."

"Can't what? What are you talking about?"

"I . . . can't hit lefty."

Coach Sharp laughed. "What are you talking about? You're a great switch-hitter. You don't think the USC coaches will be impressed when they see you? They will. Trust me, you're just as strong from the left side of the plate as you are the right."

"Coach, I can't. I'll have to bat righty."

Coach Sharp's face darkened. "I told you, you gotta stop with this goofy behavior, Sam. I mean it. I'm telling you as your coach to go bat lefty from the right side of the plate. You can do it, and I expect you to do it."

Trevor nodded, but his insides shook. He hefted his bat and staggered toward the plate. He looked over his shoulder. Coach Sharp glared at him.

Trevor stopped.

84

SAM

"He can do that?" Sam asked.

"He can do anything," McKenna said.

Dolph nodded that it was true.

"I don't know," Sam said.

"Then what's your plan?" McKenna folded her arms across her chest.

Sam nodded. "Okay, let's go. Dolph, get Wolf in there. Don't let him bite anyone."

"Wolf no bite. Only if Dolph say 'bite.'"

Sam turned to McKenna. "You get Trevor's attention in the ruckus. I'll be in the bathroom. Get him in there as fast as you can, and then you've got to keep anyone else from going in. Can you do that?"

"I'm an actress. I'll improvise."

Sam leaned over and kissed her cheek. McKenna blushed,

and they both hopped out of the car.

"Dolph," McKenna said, "give me sixty seconds before you send Wolf onto the field."

She grabbed Sam's hand, and they sprinted across the parking lot. This time it was McKenna who kissed him on the cheek.

"I better see you again," she said.

"There's no way you won't," he said.

She dashed off toward the backstop and Sam ducked into the bathroom. He opened the door of the last stall by the wall, pulled it shut, and began to remove his clothes so he could get into the uniform even faster.

85

TREVOR

Trevor stared helplessly at the coach's angry look.

"What?" Coach Sharp shouted from just outside the dugout.

"Let's go, batter." The umpire and the catcher were staring at him, too.

Trevor's stomach heaved.

He doubled over and threw up.

He heard Klum and Needum howling with laughter from the dugout. The kids in the Sherman Oaks dugout giggled, too.

The pitcher, Lee Pitts, said, "Man, that's gross."

The umpire had at least a bit of sympathy. "Kid, you okay?"

Trevor nodded and looked up.

He blinked at what he saw, and blinked again. Something big and dark leaped over the fence along the warning track in left field. The dog—it was a big dog—sprinted into the middle of the field behind second base. The dog spun around, planted itself, barked twice, then tilted its head with a tongue lolling from the side of its mouth.

There was an uproar from the crowd and the players. Trevor stared for a moment before he spoke under his breath. "Wolf?"

86

TREVOR

"Pssst!"

Trevor looked behind him.

McKenna Steele gestured wildly. "Come on. Now. Sam's in the bathroom."

Trevor looked around. No one paid any attention to him. People were pointing and laughing as the umpire circled the dog with caution. Trevor took off, slipping between a break in the backstop before the fence along the dugout began. He ducked between bleachers and dashed into the bathroom.

"See you in a minute," McKenna said.

Inside, it took a couple seconds for Trevor's eyes to adjust.

"Trevor? Is that you?" Sam's voice came from the last stall.

Trevor flung open the door and saw his twin brother

standing there in a pair of boxers.

"Hurry."

"Did you see how close that was?" Trevor asked as he shucked off his uniform. "Sharp wanted me to bat lefty! I made you proud in the field, though. You should have seen the line drive I snagged to end the inning, but I never batted lefty in my life."

"It's my fault," Sam said, tugging on the uniform pants. "I meant to tell you."

Sam pulled the top over his head and accepted the blue cap from Trevor. "Your phone's in the jeans pocket."

"Yours is in your bat bag," Trevor said.

"Great, I'm ready. We did it. I've got to go." Sam hugged him and patted his back before bolting out the door and into the sunlight.

Trevor slowly pulled on the jeans and T-shirt Sam left, wondering in the back of his mind how they'd gotten so dusty and dirty and where the big tear had come from.

After half a minute he heard the bathroom door swing open. He froze as the footsteps scratched along the concrete floor and stopped outside the stall.

"Trevor?"

87

SAM

"Here." Coach Sharp handed Sam a clump of paper towels.

"What, Coach?"

Coach Sharp pointed toward a patch of dirt just outside the batter's box. "You don't expect anyone else to mop up your puke, do you?"

"My . . ." Sam swallowed.

"Hurry up. That guy's got his dog and we're ready to go. I don't know what your problem is, Sam, but if it's gonna make you puke again, bat from the other side."

"You want me to bat lefty?"

"Don't play with me, boy. I won't say it again. This pitcher's throwing a sidearm curve with plenty on it. You want to try and stand in and hit it when it's coming right at you like that, be my guest, but if you do, we won't be winning any championship and you won't be winning that spot with USC. That's my

292

prediction, but you do what you want."

Coach Sharp turned away muttering about the puke.

Sam looked at the mess, stopped breathing through his nose, and stumbled toward the batter's box. He bent down, looked away, and scooped up as much of the puke as he could, wiping it off the dirt before the umpire told him that was fine and to get himself into the batter's box.

Sam jogged over to the on-deck circle and dumped the dirty paper towels into the trash, then stepped up to the plate, on the right side where he could bat lefty. Sam took a couple practice swings and hunkered down, eyeing the pitcher.

88

TREVOR

Trevor stayed silent until he saw a girl's feet beneath the stall door.

"McKenna?" He pushed the door open.

"We've got to go." McKenna held out her hand. "If they find out you played in the game, they'll disqualify Sam. Come on, Trevor. We can't ruin it for him."

Trevor nodded and took her hand. She led him out, stopping at the door to make sure the coast was clear. "Hurry."

She took his hand again and they dashed away from the stands and out into the parking lot. They didn't stop until they were safe inside the limo. It was then that he noticed the sad look in McKenna's eyes."

"We did it," he said. "What's wrong?"

"Trevor," she said in a quiet voice, "I have to tell you something."

89

SAM

The pitcher had a wicked side arm, and Sam couldn't recover enough from the strangeness of it to get off a good swing on the first pitch.

"Ball."

Sam got lucky. The pitch had been the curve Coach Sharp spoke of, one that would be brutal to try to hit from the other side of the plate. Now that he had a line on it, Sam knew he could tag it batting lefty.

The next pitch was all heat, but low. Sam let it pass.

"Strike!"

Sam glanced back at the umpire. He got nothing but a stony stare in return. Sam shrugged, stepped out of the box, took a couple swings, and stepped back in. The next pitch was another curve. Sam swung with everything he had. The bat connected and sent the ball flying with a solid crack.

Sam took off.

But he stopped halfway down the first-base line as the ball sailed too far to the right.

"Foul!"

Sam returned to the plate and the 1–2 count. Behind the backstop sat two men in USC hats, the coaches there to pick the MVPs. Up behind them, his dad, his real dad, waved and gave him a thumbs-up. Sam's heart swelled at the sight of his father, and he ached to hug him. Instead he gave a nod and a thumbs-up and stepped back into the box.

The pitcher wound up and threw. It was the curve, sailing way outside and glimmering with its red dot. Sam knew right where it would be when it crossed the plate. He stayed back, waiting on it, then swung with legs, hips, shoulders, arms, and wrists.

CRACK.

This time, it went straight.

This time, it was gone.

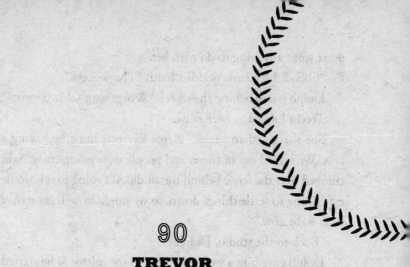

90

TREVOR

Before McKenna could speak, Trevor heard the crack of the bat and the cheer of the crowd. He let down the window, just enough to smell the hot dogs and the cut grass mixing with the warm smell of tar from the pavement.

The cheering died down.

"He must have done it," Trevor said.

Dolph opened the door with a whistle, and Wolf jumped in and sat still.

"Done what?" McKenna asked.

"Hit that pitcher batting lefty." Trevor shook his head, impressed.

"So," Trevor said, "what do you have to tell me?"

McKenna took a deep breath and let it out in a rush. "It's your mom, Trevor. Not your mom, but your biological mom."

Trevor held up a hand. "Don't, McKenna. I told Sam. I

don't want anything to do with her."

"Okay," McKenna nodded hard. "That's good."

Dolph got in behind the wheel. "Where we go, Mr. Trevor?"

Trevor looked at McKenna.

She shrugged and said, "Pierce Everette must be having a cow. We bolted out of there, and people were going crazy. Sam climbed over the fence behind the studio. It's going to take some explaining to settle things down, so we might as well get it over with right now."

"Back to the studio, Dolph."

Dolph gave him a worried glance in the mirror as he started the car.

"Dolph thinks they'll blame him," McKenna said.

"You let me worry about *them*, Dolph, you hear me? I got your back, and I appreciate your help."

Dolph grinned and pulled out of the lot.

Trevor took one more deep breath, knowing it would be a long time—if ever—before he smelled those smells again and felt the thrill of playing to win mixed with the knotted fear that you might lose.

Then he put the window up and sat back in his seat.

They got onto the highway and rode for several minutes before he asked, "Why did you look so sad when you were going to tell me about our mother, McKenna?"

McKenna's lower lip disappeared.

"Well, you can tell me why without telling me who, right?"

"I guess."

"Okay," Trevor said. "Why?"

"Well, she's gone, Trevor."

298

"She left the country?" Trevor tilted his head.

"No. Gone, gone."

Trevor felt suddenly cold. "You mean, dead, gone?"

McKenna nodded. "I'm sorry, Trevor. That's why I thought you'd want to know."

Trevor felt like the seat were gone from underneath him, as if he were floating. Pain pierced his heart in a spot he hadn't even known was there.

91

SAM

After Sam's home run, Lee Pitts struck out Dorian Klum and sent the Blue Sox back into the field.

Sam played well on defense, helping with a double play and fielding a pop fly. Still, the Sherman Oaks team was able to score another run, so Coach Sharp put Klum on the mound at the end of the third inning, even though the plan had been to let Graham pitch three full innings before Klum took over.

Dorian did his thing. He put down the last two Sherman Oaks batters with just nine pitches. Sam watched the USC coaches talking to one another after the last pitch of the inning, a fastball that must have been close to eighty miles an hour, and he knew he'd have to do something special at bat if he was going to beat Klum for the MVP.

That's just what he did. In the bottom of the fourth, Sam got up and blasted a second home run to tie the score. His team went crazy, and as Sam stepped on home plate after rounding the bases, he couldn't help grinning to himself. The three USC coaches all had their eyes on him as they whispered to one another.

Klum kept the pressure on. He hit a solid double, blasting a line drive into the hole between left and center field. Pitts kept pitching and finished the inning without giving up another run. Klum put three down with fourteen pitches to end the inning. In the fifth Sherman Oaks put in a fresh pitcher, a redheaded kid with freckles who looked like a stork but threw like a bull, and the inning was scoreless for both teams, even though the Blue Sox worked through the rest of their lineup.

There were two outs in the fifth when Sam stepped up to the plate. He wanted to hit three home runs and thought that if he did, it would lock up his spot with the USC coaches. The stork had a changeup that Sam bit on, swinging and missing. He let the next pitch by because it almost hit the plate—ball. The third pitch was a fastball outside. Sam swung for the fences and connected. He started down the first-base line only to watch the ball drift outside the post in right field. The foul ball left him with a 1–2 count.

Sam grit his teeth and hunkered down. The next pitch was way inside but burning fast. Sam stepped back and took the ball. On a 2–2 count, the stork threw another changeup. Sam tried to hold back, but he'd already committed to the swing. He connected with a crack, and the ball took off. Sam sprinted for first, keeping an eye on the ball as it started to come down. The left fielder ran for the fence.

It would be a close call.

92

SAM

The ball fell inside the fence.

Sam rounded second as the left fielder scooped up the ball and made an amazing throw to third. The third-base coach waved Sam off. He stopped on a dime and raced back for second. The third baseman rifled it to second. Sam dove and touched the bag just as the tag came down.

"Safe!" the umpire shouted from home plate.

Sam got up and dusted off. He was the potential go-ahead run, and Dorian Klum was up.

Sam wanted to win, badly, but a part of him couldn't help not wanting Klum to get a hit. With two hits and the way he pitched, Klum just might edge Sam out for the MVP.

Klum didn't make Sam wait. He blasted the first pitch over the second baseman's head. Sam rounded third and dug in for home. Maybe it was the thought of Klum winning the game that made him hesitate, maybe it was the skill with which the right fielder scooped up the ball. The third-base coach screamed at Sam to keep going.

Sam found his speed again and lowered his head. The throw came in. Sam slid into the plate for the lead in a cloud of dust.

Before the dust even settled, the umpire shouted, "Safe!"

The team went wild, and Coach Sharp had to bark at them to settle down so they could finish the inning. They still had to keep Sherman Oaks from scoring in the top of the final inning if they were going to win, and they had to win. If they didn't, neither Sam nor Klum would have to worry about being MVP. Only the winning team's MVP would go to the USC Elite Training Center.

The next Blue Sox batter went down swinging. Dorian Klum and the rest of the defense would have to keep Sherman Oaks from scoring another run. Dorian put the first two batters down, pitching like a demon. The third batter stepped into the box, and Sam's stomach was in knots. If Klum struck him out, too, it would be hard for the USC coaches not to make him MVP.

With all his might, Sam wished for the batter to hit the ball—not just any hit, but a hit Sam could field.

On a 1–1 count, Sam's wish came true.

A low, fast grounder zipped past Klum's ankles on its way up the middle of the infield.

Now all Sam had to do was make the play.

93

SAM

Sam didn't even think; he reacted. He dove for the ball, stretching with all his might. He just snagged the grounder.

As he slid over the dirt, Sam snatched the ball from his own glove, twisted, and threw to first. The ball smacked into Frankie's glove just as the batter crossed the base.

"You're out!" the umpire shouted, jerking his thumb up in the air.

It was an amazing play and a fantastic victory.

Sam knew he had a chance to win the MVP, but Dorian had pitched so well that it really was only a chance. Dorian's fastball was as good as any twelve-year-old's Sam had ever heard of, and Dorian's hitting—something Sam counted on to be average only—had been outstanding on this day.

While Sam celebrated with his team, slapping backs and trading hugs, he felt like he was back in the studio, acting. All he could really think about was getting the MVP and a spot in the USC Elite Training Center. Dorian appeared to be thinking about it, too. The big pitcher had removed a comb from his bat bag and ran it through his hair, maybe so he'd look good in the picture-taking that would come with winning the award.

The USC coaches—all three of them, including Coach Cruz—gathered together around home plate, talking in low voices to one another in an obvious debate. Sam could tell the other two disagreed about who should be the MVP. They both finally looked at Coach Cruz and shrugged, apparently leaving the decision up to him.

Sam and his team shook hands with the Sherman Oaks players before lining up down the first-base line near home plate. They stood at attention as Coach Cruz emerged from the group of coaches with the three-foot-high MVP trophy. Only Frankie Schmelling stood between Sam and Dorian Klum.

Coach Cruz walked their way and offered Sam a small smile. But something was wrong with the smile. Sam knew what when Coach Cruz stopped walking.

The smile for Sam had been the smile you give someone you feel bad for.

The coach looked away from Sam, stopped directly in front of Dorian Klum, and cleared his throat to speak.

94

SAM

Like everyone else, Sam knew he wasn't going to get the MVP.

Dorian grinned so hard it looked like his face was a balloon ready to burst. Unable to contain the incredible glee of his victory over Sam, he leaned behind Frankie, made a fist, and whispered, "You suck so bad, Palomaki. I told you I'd be MVP!"

The pure hatred and rudeness shocked Sam, even though he knew Klum well. What shocked him even more was when Frankie bent down to tie his shoe and Klum's fist stuck up in the air for everyone to see, including the USC coaches.

Coach Cruz's expression changed from joy to disgust as he stared at Klum's fist until the pitcher realized what had happened, went red-faced, and tucked his arm away behind his own back.

With a firm nod of his head, Coach Cruz held up the trophy

for the crowd to see and spoke in a voice they all could hear. "Ladies and gentlemen, please join me in congratulating the Blue Sox MVP and winner of one of the prestigious spots in our USC Elite Training Center. We all know there are no guarantees, but we also know that many, even most, of our Training Center graduates go on to become not only part of the USC baseball program but then to play in the pros. For most young players, it's a dream come true. The center is a place not only for the most skilled players but for players with *character*, who embody everything good about the game. So, I'm very happy to give this award today . . ."

Dorian stepped forward, reaching for the trophy.

That's when Coach Cruz sidestepped the big pitcher, keeping the trophy well away from him.

". . . to Sam Palomaki."

95
SAM

"Impressive." Sam's father stretched his neck and angled his nose up to take in the full height of the gates as they passed through.

Dolph glanced in the rearview mirror and offered Sam a smile.

The limo pulled into the circle and came to stop at the bottom of the front steps. Dolph hurried around the car and opened the door. Sam slipped out and they climbed the steps. Thomas, the butler, stood waiting at the top, unable to hold back a grin.

"Master . . . Sam," he said, his eyes flickering at Sam's dad.

Sam's dad held out his hand. Thomas hesitated, then shook it.

"Thanks for taking care of my son," Sam's dad said.

"Please," Thomas said, regaining his composure and opening the front doors. "Everyone is waiting."

They followed the butler through the house. Sam's dad didn't bother to hide his amazement at the towering entryway, the sculptures, paintings, and elegant furniture. Sam was surprised when Thomas led them all the way through the house only to find the pool area abandoned. When Trevor said a party out back, Sam assumed it would be a few people around the pool with some fancy food.

Thomas saw his confusion and pointed at the steps leading down through the gardens and into the trees. Sam and his dad followed, all the way through the leafy canopy and out onto the lush and spacious lawn.

"Wow," Sam said, staring.

In front of them, in the middle of the lawn, a tent—no, a pavilion—rose up to a point that nearly outreached the trees. At its peak, a red pennant waved in the breeze. Music from a string quartet and the buzz of voices floated across the grass. They walked along a red carpet and entered the tent between two thick columns supporting a flowered arch above the opening.

The carpet ran through the tent's center, and at the far end a long table sat raised up above the rest. Sitting at the center place was Trevor's dad. On one side sat Trevor's mom, busy texting. Trevor and McKenna were next to her. On the other side of Trevor's dad were two empty chairs. When Trevor's dad saw Sam and his father, the Hollywood power broker rose up from his spot and held his hands out to ask for everyone's attention.

A crowd of people stood by their chairs around circular tables bursting with flowers and glittering with silver, crystal, and china place settings. A handful at a time, they followed the sight line of Trevor's dad and grew quiet with curiosity, staring at Sam and his dad. Finally, the entire crowd was staring at them, some pointing and whispering quietly to their neighbors.

Sam felt very alone until his father put a hand on his shoulder, and Sam saw from his expression that his father didn't know quite what to do, either. Sam saw Trevor smile at him and offer up a big wink. McKenna grinned as well and pointed to the two empty chairs at the end of the raised table.

Thomas took Sam's dad by the arm, breaking their frozen pose, and led them through the whispering crowd to the table in front, where he mounted the steps and pulled out the chairs at their places.

Before they could sit down, Trevor's father raised his glass and spoke so that everyone could hear. "As you all know, we're here to begin a project that will keep many of us very busy for the next twelve months. And, while I'm sure the project we all know as *Dark Cellar* will be a blockbuster, this is a pretty extravagant party for a movie that has yet to earn a dime."

Everyone laughed politely. Trevor's dad smiled until silence fell again. Sam caught many of the people stealing looks at him and then Trevor, comparing the two.

"But this is a special project. I knew that from the moment I read the script. There's a passion in this story that's off the charts. Then I met the writer and his son, and I knew it was meant to be. That's why this party is something more than the kickoff to a major Hollywood project."

Trevor's dad looked around at the entire crowd, smiling warmly.

"It's a homecoming, of sorts. No, the boy at my right isn't

the result of the latest three-D special effects. He's very real, and yes, he looks exactly like our son, Trevor.

"Please allow me to introduce you, and the world, to our son's brother, Sam. Sam is the son of Randall and Mary Palomaki. . . . They are biological brothers, identical twins, two boys separated at birth, but back together now.

"And I want you all to know that they—and *we*—are *not* friends. . . ."

Sam swallowed.

Trevor's dad raised his glass even higher. His eye twinkled at Sam.

It was Trevor's mom now who put a hand on her husband's arm so that she could finish his sentence. She smiled warmly at Sam.

In a voice everyone could hear, she said, "That's right; we're family."

PINCH HIT

Pinch Hit Q&A with Tim Green

Game-Changing Pinch Hitters

A Sneak Peek at *Force Out*

Pinch Hit Q&A with Tim Green

Trevor loves to act but he also has a passion for baseball. Do you think young athletes should have multiple hobbies and interests besides just sports?

I think kids should definitely feel comfortable pursuing several interests outside of sports. You never know how you're going to develop as an athlete or a musician or a math student or a public speaker unless you give it a try. So if you're passionate about something, it's important for you to follow it and try to develop your talents in that area. Great opportunities might arise from those other interests.

Trevor experiences a bad case of nerves before stepping up to bat, just like Sam gets nervous before filming his scene in the movie. What advice do you have for athletes who get nervous before games?

First of all, it's natural to get nervous—that only means you care about the outcome of the game. Different people have different ways to deal with their nerves, but the most effective way for me has always been to read a good book right before the game. A book takes you away to another time and another place. I used to read before every athletic contest and every test because it put me in a calm state of mind. You may not be able to read a book during the game, but at that point, the comfort comes from the perspective you gained from the book, knowing things are going to be okay.

Sometimes there can be a lot of bad talk and bickering between opposing teams or even between teammates, like when Dorian Klum insults Trevor after he strikes out. What do you think players should do if they find themselves in this situation?

As a baseball coach myself, I don't like that kind of negativity. Not between opponents, and especially not between teammates. It shouldn't go on. A good coach should be aware of what's happening between players and stop that kind of behavior. But if one of your teammates is still being negative, you should talk to that teammate head-on and say, "I'm doing the best I can do, and I know you're doing the best you can do, and if we're going to have success as a team, we need to help each other out as teammates."

At the end of *Pinch Hit*, the USC coaches see Klum being mean to Sam, and it affects their opinion of him. What are some qualities that coaches look for in their prospective athletes besides great athletic ability?
Coaches want players who are winners on and off the field. Players who fight to the very end of every game and don't give up. Players who support their teammates in times of adversity. As you move up to the higher levels of sports, it's even more important for a team to act as a team. Because when you play college sports or go to the pros, everyone is great, that's a given. So it's those little things that make the difference, like being positive and team-oriented and a leader during and after the game. A coach wants a player who is willing to sacrifice his or her own best interests so that the team can succeed.

***Pinch Hit* draws inspiration from Mark Twain's classic novel, *The Prince and the Pauper*. Why do you think stories about two people switching places have such timeless appeal?**
I think it's because we all like to believe that we can alter our circumstances. And I think it's because we like being reminded that we make our own happiness in our lives based on who we are on the inside and how we interact with the people around us—it's not dependent upon our setting. Yes, it's fun for Sam to live in a mansion, but ultimately he realizes that what he really wants is the love of his dad and to be a great baseball player, and he also wants McKenna's friendship. Those things don't depend upon living on a mansion. And it's not the mansion that Trevor misses. He misses the fun things about his life and his family. Finally, I think another reason these stories continue to have appeal is that there's a mischief maker in all of us, and let's be honest, we all think it's fun to trick adults (in a harmless way, of course).

Game-Changing Pinch Hitters

A pinch hitter is a player who steps in to bat in place of another player. They may not be as famous as Babe Ruth or Hank Aaron, but these five professional pinch hitters all played major roles for their teams.

- Kirk Gibson of the Los Angeles Dodgers could barely walk due to injuries in both of his legs, but he was determined to make a difference in game one of the 1988 World Series. With the Dodgers down 4–3 in the bottom of the ninth, Gibson came off the bench to pinch hit for Alejandro Pena, and hit the game-winning home run for a 5–4 victory over the Oakland Athletics. This play is now considered one of the greatest home runs of all time.
- With 212 pinch hits, Lenny Harris holds the record* for the most pinch hits in a major league baseball career. Lenny has played nearly every position, except for pitcher or catcher.
- John Vander Wal holds the record* for the most pinch hits in a single season—he had twenty-eight pinch hits for the Colorado Rockies in 1995. He retired after the 2004 season and began coaching younger players on the skills of hitting.
- Manny Mota was a pinch-hit pro for the Los Angeles Dodgers and was often called upon in late innings to help save the day. He was especially good against left-handed pitchers and had the unique ability to hit perfect line drive singles.
- In 1892, Tom Daly of the Brooklyn Dodgers was sent to pinch hit for Hub Collins and hit the first pinch hit home run in major league history to tie the game with Boston in the ninth inning. He then brought in another run in the tenth inning, but Boston still came away with the 8–7 win.

* Records as of July 2012

**Don't miss Tim Green's
next exciting baseball book!**

1

When it came to his best friend, Joey would do just about anything. He listened quietly to the sound of his parents getting ready for bed and waited impatiently for his father to turn off the late news on their bedroom television. Noise drained from the house like used bathwater, leaving nothing but the tick of Joey's small, battery-operated alarm clock. Even Martin, his little brother, lay still in the nursery.

It was time.

If Mr. Kratz had been holding Joey's own summer hostage, he would never have crept from his bed, dressed, paused in the bathroom for a secret ingredient, and then slipped down the stairs through the empty rooms. But he wasn't doing this for himself. He was doing it for Zach. He and Zach shared the same dream. It was a baseball dream, and one they planned on realizing together.

It wasn't fair, that was for sure. Mr. Kratz was the toughest

1

teacher in sixth grade. It wasn't just his dark, hairy knuckles and the way he snuffled and snorted at the beginnings and ends of his sentences. Stories of Mr. Kratz's mind-bending tests, backbreaking homework, and failing final grades crept all the way down into the elementary school, rivaling Snow White's evil witch, Jack's giant, and Cinderella's stepmother. Joey escaped most of Mr. Kratz's thick-browed scowls by working harder than almost anyone in science class, but Zach wasn't put together that way. Either things came easily to Zach, or he seemed to have little use for them.

Throughout the year, Zach fell short, and throughout the year, Mr. Kratz gathered his bulk by adjusting the big leather belt he wore as a boundary between his massive upper and lower body and warned Zack—along with a surprising portion of the rest of the class—that failure meant summer school. No exceptions.

Everyone knew about Mr. Kratz's field lab on the last Saturday before the end of school. That famous trip by the morning train to the Beaver River Biological Field Station often tilted the balance between passing and failing the class because of the extra credit you got for going. When Mr. Kratz heard the news about the Little League championship game being held on the same day as his field trip, he snorted, rumbled, and asked, "What's that got to do with me?"

Mr. Kratz loved Beaver River. The floppy felt hat he wore every day came from the field station's gift shop, purchased more than thirty years ago when Mr. Kratz was a college student with dreams of scientific fame. Maybe that's why Mr. Kratz possessed such a heavy scowl—because long ago his dreams of Nobel prizes or being on the cover of *Science* magazine had been sent to bed without any supper.

In the back corner of the fridge, Joey found a ziplock bag. He fiddled around, doctoring up its contents, then crammed the bag into the pocket of his jeans before slipping into the garage. Joey's garage smelled like concrete. The sound of his feet scuffing across the floor filled the darkness. He located a second baggie on his father's workbench and tucked that into his back pocket along with a flat-head screwdriver.

He then lifted his bike over the threshold of the side door before walking it down the driveway. He avoided the bright cone of light from the streetlight that marked the line between his yard and the Guthries' next door. With a final glance back at his quiet house, Joey mounted the bike and took off into the night. The thrill of the darkness, the quiet, and breaking the rules fueled his pumping legs. The clank of gears only increased his speed. Like a rocket, he shot past the low stone walls marking the entrance to his development.

It wasn't often people turned left out of Windward because Windward was the last major home development before the roads turned rural and the homes were a hodgepodge of run-down saltboxes, trailers, and old farmhouses, bent and staggering under the weight of time. After Windward, things quickly turned country.

County Road 347 went due south, and if you kept on it for several miles, you'd run smack-dab into the Bickford State Forest Preserve. If you followed 347 and its eastward jog around the forest, you'd see a red mailbox marking the long dirt road that led to a cabin tucked away in the woods like a hidden kingdom for wood elves, fairies, or goblins. Joey knew where Mr. Kratz lived because Joey's mother had been a customer for years, buying lots of the great man's wild blackberry jam and a case of his honey at the end of each summer.

Joey pumped his legs in the dark, keeping to the shoulder of the road and shivering at the inky blackness between the trees on either side of the road. Above, the light of a full moon struggled through a thick mist like a flashlight behind a bedsheet. Droplets almost too small to matter had begun to drift down, and they tickled Joey's face if he held up his chin. At the corner where Route 347 met Cherry Valley Road stood an abandoned church with a steeple stripped of its paint by time and whitened by the sun. The empty socket where a bell once hung stared down at Joey, and the doorless entrance gaped wide like an ogre's mouth. Joey slowed and got down off his bike, walking it into the weedy lot where churchgoers long ago probably parked their wagons.

"Zach?" Joey's voice died quickly in the mist. He cleared his throat and barked louder. "Zach, are you here?"

No reply, and that annoyed him because Zach was always late. He peered down Cherry Valley Road in the direction of Zach's house, straining his eyes and huffing impatiently. Then he froze. From inside the pit of that empty doorway came the sound of groaning, creaking floorboards.

The hair on Joey's neck jumped to attention. Goose bumps riddled his arms. He opened his mouth to scold Zach, but if it was Zach inside the church, his bike should be somewhere, standing in the weeds. There was no bike in the moonlight.

Joey's mind spun like a top. Had their secret plan been

4

discovered? Had Zach spilled the beans? If so, who was in the church?

"Hey!"

The voice coming from the belly of the church was low and gruff. Fear grabbed Joey by the throat because he could think of only one person who it might be: Kratz, the giant ogre.

The footsteps kept coming, stomping now.

A figure stirred in the deep shadows of the doorway. Joey's brain screamed to run, but his legs stood frozen in the damp weeds.

2

A shadowy figure leaped from the doorway and bolted down the steps straight for Joey. "Boo!"

Joey shrieked and his legs found their way. He dropped his bike and bolted for the road. His feet hit the pavement, heading for home, when the mad cackling from the church steps became a howl of delight.

Joey spun and screamed. "Zach! Are you nuts? Are you kidding? I'm out here in the middle of the night to try and save your butt and you're goofing around?"

Zach staggered toward him, wiping the tears from his eyes and snaking an arm around Joey's neck, hugging him close and shaking with delight.

Finally Zach's laughter subsided enough for him to speak. "Did you . . . did you pee your pants, bro?"

"Stop laughing. It's not that funny."

"You had to hear your voice. Bro, you were killing me." Zach caught his breath and let out a ragged and satisfied sigh. Black hair spiked the top of his head, as always, and his small dark eyes gathered enough of the hidden moon to light up. "Awesome."

"Where's your bike, anyway?"

Zach walked over to the corner of the small wooden building, reached into the damp weeds, and righted his machine. "It's soaked, bro."

"Good, so's mine." Joey raised his own bike, his voice dripping with disgust. "Now let's go."

Joey pumped his pedals and burned off the annoyance he felt at Zach's foolery. The mist built up on his face so that he had to lick his lips and wipe his eyes. The road stayed dark and except for the quiet click of their bike sprockets and hiss of their tires on the wet pavement, they might have been in a silent dream. They pedaled without speaking for a couple of miles, winding through the trees, up and down hills until they came to a dirt cut in the road and the red mailbox.

Joey got off his bike and Zach copied him.

"Man, is that creepy." Zach stared at the hole in the trees where the dirt road quickly melted away. Spanish moss hung in limp strands, and evil little nooks and crannies infected the trunks and limbs of the twisted old trees leaning out and over the dirt driveway.

"I don't think he even has electricity." Joey spoke in a whisper. Even though it felt like he and Zach were the only two people on the planet, he knew Mr. Kratz lay—hopefully asleep—in the heart of this darkness, tucked into a snug corner of his cabin like an overgrown weevil.

Zach shook his head. "Guy is such a freak."

Joey hid his bike into the wild hedge on the other side of the road.

"You don't want to ride?" Zach asked, even though he

followed Joey's lead.

Joey crossed the road and started down the path. "This driveway is too bumpy. We're better off walking."

Zach stayed close, and quickly the moonlight was gone. Joey took the cell phone from his pocket, opened it, and used its meager light to avoid the biggest ruts and stones. It seemed like forever, but finally a fuzzy patch of light appeared and Mr. Kratz's cabin materialized. Joey pocketed the phone and stopped at the edge of the small clearing. The barn loomed even bigger than Joey remembered it, dwarfing the log cabin. Between the two buildings, Mr. Kratz's rusty red compact pickup slept like a guard dog in a dirt patch.

Zach shivered. "Oh, man."

Even a whisper sounded too loud, so Joey barely spoke.

"You should have studied for the last test like I told you." Joey bit down on his lower lip, scared and angry that he was even here doing this.

"I *tried*. Not everybody's as smart as you," Zach hissed quietly in Joey's ear. "Is this gonna work?"

"You got a better idea?" Joey asked in a hushed voice.

Zach shook his head, and Joey crept forward toward the pickup truck and into the pale light of the moon. Joey studied the setting carefully, looking for any kind of movement and listening for any sound. The homestead was still and lifeless. From his back pocket, he removed the screwdriver and the baggie from his father's workbench. He knelt down in front of the truck, took one final look around, then lay on his back in the dirt and squirmed underneath the engine.

Zach squirmed in beside him and without speaking. Joey

8

opened his phone and handed it to Zach, pointing at the fuel pump where he wanted the light. Joey fumbled with the clamp he'd taken from his father's workbench, fished it around the fuel line, then inserted the loose end into the little collar and began to cinch it down with the screwdriver. Zach's breathing grew heavy and excited. Joey wanted to tell him to be quiet; he was afraid of making too much noise. Being wedged in under Mr. Kratz's truck in the darkness with his legs sticking out was the scariest thing he'd ever experienced or imagined.

That was until he heard the low, guttural snarl at his feet, a wet snort, and the killer snap of big sharp teeth.

A pathetic whine escaped Zach's throat and his eyes bulged. "Joey, is that a dog?"

3

Not only was it a dog, it was one of the biggest, nastiest dogs Joey had ever seen. Kept on a thick chain fastened to an old mill wheel during the summer, the dog Mr. Kratz called Daisy snarled and slobbered and howled at Mr. Kratz's customers until he emerged from the workshop in his barn and uttered one inaudible word. Daisy then wilted like the flower he was named after.

Joey knew about the dog, but had no idea what Mr. Kratz did with it at night. That's why he'd carefully surveyed the homestead before trapping himself and his best friend under the front end of the pickup. From what he'd seen and heard, he had concluded the dog must be put inside at night.

Now he knew different.

"Joey. Oh my God." Zach was practically crying, and he grabbed Joey's wrist so that Joey had to twist it before he could yank it free.

"Let *go* of me, you bonehead."

Joey's hand snaked into his other pocket. His fingers groped for the cold baggy, yanking it free and tearing it open with his other hand. With a low whistle, he tossed a ball of ground meat out into the dirt.

"Good boy," Joey whispered. "Here, boy. Here, Daisy."

He tossed another scrap. Daisy snarled louder and sniffed the air, then padded around behind the front tire to gobble up the meat.

"That's a good boy." Joey emptied the entire baggy to the tune of snapping teeth, snorting, and slobbering.

"How much of that stuff do you have?"

"I'm out."

"Now what?" Zach asked, still paralyzed with panic.

"Relax."

Daisy paced back and forth, sniffing at their feet before he came around by the tire, gave one final snort, then lay down in the dirt so they could see his wet muzzle and the glow of front teeth. He put his head on his front paws, then rolled over on his side, twitched a bit, then began to snore.

"You killed it?" Zach asked in an excited whisper.

"No. Don't you hear it snoring?"

"Okay, let's go."

"I'm not finished."

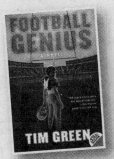